the places we've been

David Mears

Clink
Street

Published by Clink Street Publishing 2024

Copyright © 2024

First edition.

ISBN:

Restlessness before the journey begins and a minor literary obituary

This traveller is restless. It may be the prickling heat of early summer. It may be that there is indecision in the air as the seasons change. It may be that this traveller is uncertain of both times gone by and those to come.

It is a silent Sunday at home. There is a pile of unread books on a stand-up piano in the corner of the room. Above the piano are shelves framing a dense forest of coloured book spines. The titles speak of more naive times, of forgotten enthusiasms and temporary distractions, others of moments of heady aspiration. They speak of a life both lived and unlived.

Jazzlife. William Claxton. A mammoth edition of arresting, moving, engaging, direct, spontaneous portraits of a 1960s road trip across a racially segregated United States. It was a time when black and white photography mattered. Urgent and arresting. Less was more. There were no hard drives for superfluous storage or Photoshop filters or digital tricks. Jazz was cool. Players had their sax licks and chops. They used words that have freefallen out of our language. 'Cats', 'the cool', 'breezin'. The roads were open and long. Jazz players played hard, night after night. Their crowds were small and needed persuading, one by one, bar to bar, club to club. William Claxton went travelling to see it.

Other books are settled trenchantly like dust.
George Orwell. *The Road to Wigan Pier*.
Solzhenitsyn. *One Day in the Life of Ivan Denisovich*.
A fly buzzes intermittently.

This traveller is fishing in memories, casting out to catch the whisper of the opening chords of a half-remembered song. A viscose film has covered the past and muffled it beyond the reach of every day. At least for now.

So why travel? And to where?

This traveller is about to leave. It is a well-trodden path. Many travellers before him have emptied post boxes, switched off the gas supply and watered their plants before pulling a front door behind them and turning the key. Many have chewed their pencils on their way to towns with exotic names, sat in prosaic squares, glanced down half-lit alleys and drunk behind the steamed-up windows of someone else's neighbourhood bar.

Forwards, backwards, sideways. We keep on moving.

This traveller is anxious to begin, to discover if there can be an end to his sketchy idea of a narrative.

Ah yes, the narrative. Observing this traveller is this writer, his other self, wary of literary pretension, over easy word pairings and clichéd cultural cul-de-sacs. You and I? We can call it pompous prickery if you like.

There is a blank page to write on and some days ahead. He is unsure of himself and his footsteps, of where the road may lead and how it may lead back.

Because our century is not the century of either rambling narratives or journeys. We live in the fast-paced age of GPS. Our maps show lines that connect two places. We are wired to do the same, to connect ourselves to goals and objectives, to go from A to B, faster, better, more efficiently. It is the nature of our age. Forward, forward. Momentum is essential.

But we are so often uncertain of our destination. If we have nowhere to go, there is no reason to hurry and any road will take you there.

The writer inside this traveller is made uncomfortable by these probably too easy, pop lyric observations.

He thumbs a copy of John Steinbeck's, *The Grapes of Wrath*. It is starkly designed, with an all-white cover and a bright, vivid painted image of the protagonist in the bottom right-hand corner. The white cover has a small red wine stain. This writer can remember exactly where he was when the wine was spilt and who he was with. He flicks the pages and notices intensely underlined sentences and notes in the margin. The notes mean nothing now. The sentences underlined have lost their potency. They rest flaccid on the page. Time shifts our minds. What seemed important then is no longer.

Can we ever get back to the places we've been and the people we were?

There is a scribble inside the front page – a name and an address of a village in Northern Spain.

It was the summer of 1993. She was called Carmen. She left the next day and this writer never saw her again. Can she remember him?

Thirty summers have come and gone.

Another 'could-be' pop lyric.

This writer would like to edit that thought and the words that fail to express it.

It was thirty years ago. That's it.

Say it as it is. Drop the facile, curly paged Moleskine, singer songwriter slop.

This traveller is this writer.

"You can write. Just write," said my teacher.

A word about Carmen

30 years is almost half a life, time enough for life's permanently revolving doors to spin several times through deaths in the family, children, love affairs – all of it.

The crushing, relentless trickle of time means that if I met Carmen by chance today, we wouldn't recognise each other. She wouldn't know it was my curled paperback she left a mark on and that it has stood on my bookshelf for 30 years. What memories does she have? Does she remember anything at all?

There were letters between us for many months or even a year or two after. I fell in love with the spaces between the words, the incompleteness of it, the allure of questions, not answers.

But one day like any other day the letters stopped. There was no goodbye and no announcement. I just remember a grey day of fine, misty rain walking to a London tube station thinking that it had been a long time since she had written to me and I to her.

It was a kind of ending.

Beginning

It's time to turn the water off and empty the fridge. There is some blue cheese wrapped in foil, more than a few slices of decent ham and a litre of milk. I put it all into a plastic bag and leave it at the apartment door opposite mine in the hallway with a scribbled note.

'Javier. I'm going to be away for a while. It's not much but here's a few bits to eat before they go off. Cheers. David.'

Javier is my neighbour and I feel socially awkward leaving him scraps of food. He is not a dog. He doesn't even have a dog and I don't want to be seen as a disconnected but benevolent medieval lord of the manor taking pity on my estate workers. Doling out food to the neighbours could be seen as tactless and sneering. But it's practical and the speck of a grain of sand on the Bondi Beach of our circular economy challenge. On balance I resolve my moral aesthetic quandary in favour of leaving the bag.

"Be part of the change," said Barack Obama. So I am.

The teacher who told me that I could write also told me that writing has to "come from a proper place, a real one, David. No bollocks." He dressed as he spoke, in bold colours. He wore kipper ties and misfitting jackets, the chest pocket on his jacket heavily marked with vertical coloured lines left behind from divebombing ballpoint pens skidmarking on entry. He called Shakespeare a bloke and often read little extra-curric-ular pieces that I wrote – a few bad poems, some short stories and essays. He didn't have to but he did. He gave economi-cally expressed critiques, the very best kind for 14-year-olds.

"Cut a bit."

"Have an idea and go with it."

"That's fluff. I reckon you can do better."

I often thought of him later in life as I became a hired hand, writing speeches and advertising copy. On a good day when I wrote something half-decent I would have liked that slight nod of his head and his highest praise.

"That's not bad. Not bad at all."

My travel bag is light. Just a few shirts, some shorts, train-ers. I am happy, tiptoeing close to the frontier with smug, that the bag is so carefree and uncomplicated.

I don't know exactly where I'm going or for how long so I cannot prepare for anything more. What else? A notebook, some pens and my laptop. I pack a thumbed and heavily anno-tated copy of *Journey to the Alcarria* by Camilo José Cela.

I'll tell you more about the book later. And Carmen too.

One door closes

The front door has a double lock. I turn the key more deliberately than usual, listening for the second click. The doormat is in place and correctly aligned, flush to the wall, centred with the front door. It is ritualistic to fret before travelling. It is all a part of our saying goodbye. It is mid-morning and the apartment block is quiet. One flight of stairs down and I am out onto the street. I lob my bag onto the front seat of my car.

Trust me. I've thought about how to travel and why and where to. I've thought for too long. It's been in my head for more than 20 years, a hot water bottle of inertia to cuddle up to every night.

There are practical questions of course. I've never liked planes or airports. Planes go too far, too fast. There is no time to adjust and align body, mind and soul. The food is fast and my stomach usually aches before, during and after. Planes are tuna in a tin, summaries of people at their worst: massed, hurried, anxious and irritable. And then there are the smells: powerful body odour, Pringles, airport sandwiches and silent farts caused by too much bad food and low atmospheric pressure.

And I don't want to travel far. I don't need to rocket across continents and time zones. I just need to travel across Spain to some places I've already been.

Camilo José Cela went walking. In 1946 he stepped out of his house on Madrid's Calle Alcalá, walked to the central Atocha train station and a while later arrived in Guadalajara, the starting point for his journey to the Alcarria, a region around 100 kilometres to the east of Madrid.

He had no particular place to go and no reason to arrive at any given time. His sights were set on exploring. His interest was social, his gaze set on his fellow human beings living in rural near-poverty just a few years after a bitter civil war – local before global existed.

He was looking out. Me too. But I think I may be looking sideways, backwards and inside just as much.

I had always imagined that I would go walking like he did. Walking is rhythmic, you see the world close up, there is time to reflect, to stop, to stare. Slowness facilitates cheery 'good morning's' to passers-by and the potential for serendipitous meals offered by hosts along the way, anxious to share organic treats on large wooden farmhouse tables served with gargantuan slices of homemade bread, copious fruit bowls and wine poured from label-free bottles. It demands only a rucksack, sturdy boots and economy of scale in packing. A walker's vulnerability could give me significant advantage as random strangers spill their life stories and share never-to-be-repeated philosophical insights. And I would lose a few pounds and return home brown, thinner and obviously travelled.

But in the real world, heavy walking means mosquito bites, heel blisters and aching ankles. It is also inefficient. I am not sure where I'm going and I don't want to spend a long time not getting there. Romanticism belittles and laughs at efficiency. Art is in the struggle, we were taught. Is there not value in taking time to contemplate endless fields of haystacks? Would that absence of speed not unlock meaning as I travel?

I have also considered trains. Trains suggest freedom and casual, brooding encounters with interesting strangers on lonely platforms and in half-abandoned sandwich bars. French films pull heavily on the romance of trains. And we pull on French films for romance to escape Anglo-Saxon prosaicism. On trains, we look dreamingly out of misted-up windows and stumble to buffet cars to order strong coffee and croissants. We exchange meaningful nods with others. Trains slide easily across tracks uniting destinations.

But some of the places I'm thinking of travelling to don't have stations, connections are poor and trains infrequent.

So I'm not going to follow in anyone's footsteps, not even Camilo's. His writing is my inspiration but I don't want to follow in his physical, geographical tracks.

And haven't writers done that many times before? Isn't *In the footsteps of... (insert important historical name here)* a publishing industry standard?

Hannibal.

Marco Polo.

No. This is my germination of an idea and I'm sticking to it.

So where to?

I clunk the car door behind me and look across at the passenger seat. My new and specially purchased rucksack is sleek, black and as satisfying to my ego as any personal accoutrement I possess. My former therapist would have encouraged accessing a stream of consciousness about this revelation that a simple rucksack could reinforce self-worth to such an extent. How fragile we are.

I type in P-a-k-l on the GPS.

Wrong.

Then P-a-m-p-l-o

My machine knows what I mean. My machine knows what I am thinking before I can articulate myself in written form.

Pamplona.

I could make a droll observation about the conflicts we face between machine learning, pre-destination, free choice and our intrinsic desire for freedom. But the observation may well be 50 years too late. My GPS knows where I'm going and how I'm going to get there. And the GPS is not the only universal technology to which we have ceded control.

Back to the data. Pamplona is 457 kilometres and 4 hours 39 minutes northeast from where I'm starting out in my mountain home town to the west of Madrid. The route is set and I'm not thinking anymore, or at least not about the route.

If you know Spain, you will know that that number of kilo-metres north from Madrid means another country. Landscape shifts from yellow to green. The flatlands turn hilly. Accents will shift. People from the South may tell you that the further north you go the drier and less friendly people become. People from the North may tell you that people from the South are lazy and spend too much time having fun when they could be working.

Tribes offer us crumbs of identity comfort and are as old as human beings themselves. And it may just be that they are proliferating as our largest ever global human population splinters into factions, mudslinging over ideologies, politics, sexuality, identity, borders, religion, economics and resources. Or maybe it's just that we get to hear more about it than previous generations because of that thing vibrating and pinging all day in our pockets.

On and off the road

I am out of the city now and I need a coffee. I have moved beyond IKEA, industrial estates and dormitory suburbs. The forest of streetside signage has thinned to occasional faded hoardings advertising hotels that closed years ago.

There is a petrol station up ahead so I pull in, parking underneath the corrugated iron canopy to keep my car in the shade on what is now a hot day.

The bar is dark and a fruit machine bleeps in the corner. There is a loud T.V. The coffee is strong. Service is matter of fact and efficient. There are no superfluous 'please's and 'thank you's. It is a transaction, – which is what it is. I like this stripped-down, dignified, honest recognition of what we are here for and what we are not here for.

Above the bar there are yellowing colour photographs of Spanish bar staples: squid, garlic prawns, potato omelette and a near infinite choice of sandwich combinations – ham, bacon, cheese, bacon and cheese, ham and cheese, cheese and tomato...

The sandwiches all look the same. The photographer shot them from above so we actually only see the bread. It's beyond satire and practically Warhol.

Behind the bar there is a plastic Virgin doll. She perches, legs akimbo, over a fridge next to a poster advertising seven-day winter breaks in Benidorm for 334,00 Euros (transport and hotel included).

The coffee is strong and thick. It's a Spanish truth that the smaller the village, the stronger the coffee. I order a juice too, which in Spain happily means fresh-squeezed oranges as opposed to a brightly coloured orange liquid full of chemical toxicity and an old-style EU sugar mountain served from a plastic bottle.

The barman clatters spoons from improbable heights onto saucers laid out symmetrically on the bar. He is dressed in stock issue black trousers and a short-sleeved white cotton shirt. His shirt is three-buttons open, revealing a gold chain that bounces from side to side doing the tango in happy harmony with his brisk movements. Other travellers will be passing through and they will want coffee too, and a battery of cups, saucers, spoons and sachets of sugar is ready for them. Every minute or so this master of multi-tasking pushes back the forward leaning quiff in his hair while giving orders to the kitchen, cranking out coffee from the machine, maintaining multiple conversations and handing out change to paying customers, all at the same time.

Outside the window the sky is summertime blue, as uniform as a Pantone colour reference swab. The sun is now shining harder, shadows are shortening and the day is stretching out ahead.

Back in the car and overstimulated by coffee I get to thinking about where I'm going to stay tonight. Thinking means overthinking.

It is, I think, (another) new low watermark for me, me, the previously inveterate believer in the romance of travel. What's wrong with chance?

What's wrong is that we live in data-driven times. Our routes are largely pre-determined, we read peer reviews and ascribe stars to our travel experiences. We are the jury on an out-of-body experience and we exercise our muscle to move the finger of public opinion. We see the pictures on social media, we watch the videos online, we've seen the movies and read the books. We are better informed than ever, as prepared for travel as a supermarket pizza for the oven. And I am another victim, panicked by an absence of information and the possibility of a cavity of uncertainty opening up.

Could I have made my first grave, strategic road-trip error? What happens if Pamplona is full tonight? What if the Annual Leather Manufacturers' Association has rolled into town and taken over every hotel bed with eager executives and travelling salespeople plying their trade in whips, boots and belts?

Sounds kinky but I need to sleep and I like large beds and clean showers. I gave up on "*hostales*" years ago after an intense nocturnal experience with two sex workers, one unidentified man, one broken door lock, two local police officers and a small quantity of cocaine.

And yes, I can explain everything.

I was fast asleep in a not very nice Sevillian hostel room. I had half-closed the door but not locked it (that's the broken lock bit). At around 4am I woke up to the sound of two female voices in my room. More asleep than awake, I could see two ladies, not wearing much, had walked straight in and were standing at the end of my bed talking to me about something. Something, I know, is not a powerful descriptor. But it was something and definitely not nothing and I had no idea what that something was. At this time my Spanish was non-existent. After 30 seconds or so they left the room and went further down the corridor, guessing rightly that I was probably not the man they had come to see. After a few minutes some shouting came from down the corridor. They were clearly not at all happy with the guy in the other room. Just a few moments later a man came running down the corridor, his trousers in his hands. 'Leaving' is an elegant verb to describe his drunken, lurching scamper down the narrow corridor. A small transparent plastic bag full of white powder fell from his trouser pocket just as he passed me.

After he passed by the same two ladies then ran past me chasing after him.

"*Hijo de puta*," they shouted.

I learnt at school that the best place to be when there is a punch-up is somewhere else. The scared, sweaty schoolboy inside my fake grown-up man facade took charge. I half-closed the door hoping that two centimetres of cheap plywood would create a sufficient barrier between me and the crime scene. The commotion downstairs on the street continued. I could hear a siren wailing. A blue flashing light lit up my room like a school disco. The shouting carried on, another police car came, more people came out of neighbouring doorways to watch. Across the street there was a man like me, looking down from his bedroom.

Like him, I was all good, safe in my room looking down on the scene below. Except I wasn't.

Just a few minutes later there was a knock on my door. The knock was cursory as two police officers walked directly in.

At this point it became clear that my rudimentary Spanish was going to fall short. I had worked out a few things from context. I summarise for you here in bullet-point form like one of those final slides in a corporate PowerPoint:

- Something not good had happened down the corridor.
- The police wanted to know why I had white powder all over the floor in my room.
- They wanted to understand what my connection was to the fleeing man and the two ladies.

I was of course unable to explain my emphatically periph-eral role in the drama and it felt like the wrong time to trial my newly learnt sentences from the 'Ordering in a restaurant' module of my Spanish language textbook. All I could do was to exercise my right to stay silent. Not so much a right, in fact, which implies some choice, more a simple, grim, dysfunc-tional linguistic reality.

After a few minutes that felt like hours of unclarifying dialogue, a full room inspection, a collection of samples and transfer of white powder from my hotel room floor into a plastic bag, I got dressed and went downstairs accompanied by two police officers.

Four hours and multiple disjointed declarations and con-versations later, I emerged a free man from a local police sta-tion. There was no media scrum and no Foreign Office state-ment but in my own way I enjoyed the self-righteous moment of release and vindication in the eyes of the law. Later, with a black coffee and cigarette in a nearby bar, I silently drafted my own imaginary press release.

"I am delighted to say that I have this morning been uncon-ditionally discharged by police in Sevilla. I would like to pay tribute to their professionalism etc. etc..."

I actually have no idea what was kicking off that night or who was doing what to who and why. It did involve money, sex and drugs. If there was any rock n' roll I didn't hear it and in the end I think it became apparent that my cluelessness with language was not a ruse. It was just cluelessness.

All of this is to tell you that these days I prefer hotels with doors that lock.

Behind that locked door and at my comfort-driven age I also like to see large beds, clean sheets, decent-sized bath-rooms and a window that opens so I don't have to lie awake at night stressing about noisy, hyperactive air conditioning or heating systems and their capacity to recycle killer viruses.

Writing this I realise that I am a wimp and a fraud and not worthy of the name 'traveller'. I also realise that I have a small sliver of pith, from the orange juice, stuck in one of my upper molars. It distracts me quite seriously from my own impending no-hotel road movie.

I must be more rational. I must grow up. There will be hotel rooms. There always are. And if not, I can move a few miles to a nearby town. The panic passes and I recommit to this project of discovery, excitement and not knowing where I'm going to sleep tonight or with who.

My trip would actually have to be of the late '60s hallucinatory variety, rather than this modest road-trip to engage with that last thought. I'll sleep happily on my own. I'm not on the lookout for casual sex encounters. You can't be when you're too busy adjusting the blinds and battling with the bedside Anglepoise lamp to read properly. And there's a long day ahead tomorrow. And it's been a long car drive. And my knee is creaking and after a few glasses of wine you know how it is and... and... and...

Much more likely, I'll find myself in a neighbourhood bar, smoking on an outside terrace, drinking "*patxaran*" and striking up meaningful conversation with a couple on the next table who turn out to be American university profs passing through in search of Hemingway.

It will be a ménage à trois of sorts, although a sexually limp one, as we discuss American cultural and economic imperialism in the 20th century, the ethics of bullfighting and earnestly explore the challenges and contradictions of cultural appropriation.

Did I just say Hemingway? We'll probably talk about him as well.

Time passes quickly and I start to feel hungry. I'm 150 kilometres away still and I don't feel like waiting. And I like the ritual of roadside bars. I like the corrugated iron canopies and the sense of transience and anonymity. All of us are just passing through. That, for a moment, strikes me as having the potential to be a deep thought. Any thoughts of your own on roadside bars as baby-sized metaphors for life?

Maybe not.

I did say potential deep thought.

More mundanely, the scrambled egg with prawns and garlic is exceptional. So is the slug of red wine and slab of bread. I can see through the open door into the kitchen and I watch a lady wearing a hairnet doing the cooking on her own. She moves slowly around the kitchen looking fully in control of her craft, busy but not rushed. Her white apron is immaculately clean and from what I can see so is the kitchen. It is a magisterial study in doing something limited, but very well. Airport bookshelves bend under the weight of books by people who went to Harvard once explaining how we can all do that. Save your money and just come to this bar 150 kilometres south of Pamplona. You'll have more fun too.

When the waiter asks me if I'd like anything else I could happily order the same again.

Emboldened by the meal, I decide that I must stop being a wimp. I determine to own the city on my arrival as God in his own country, to drive straight to the heart of the city centre, park right outside an inviting hotel door, sling my car key to a tall, handsome concierge and head straight to the bar for another glass or six of red wine.

But the entrance to Pamplona, I quickly discover, is another metaphor for life, a messy tripwired web of traffic lights, zebra crossings and roundabouts. It is a slow-moving sequence of stops and starts, of near misses, bumps, scrapes and major to minor irritations, and not in the Cole Porter sense. Progress is slower than I would like. Our heroic notions fizzle like the soap suds of cheap washing-up liquid as we sit in the traffic jam of piled-up human aspirations.

Soon I am in a one-way system of intricate streets in the middle of the old town. And it's obvious I shouldn't be. I am driving dangerously close to streetside café terraces and I am being stared at. A couple of pedestrians wave, but not to say hello. I wind the window down.

"¿Aquí no se puede pasar en coche, no?" (You can't come up here in a car, can you?)

"No. Te multan." (No. You'll get a fine).

This is going wrong.

I turn a corner to try and extricate myself but this time I find myself going up a one-way street when I should be going down. There's no space to turn round and I can't reverse back down the road. It's very narrow and busy with pedestrians, all of them keen not to end the day in hospital after being carved down by a saloon-driving itinerant traveller who really should have known better.

I have no-one to blame but errrrr... the government. It is only a dark, oppressive and overbearing state, I rant to myself, that could sanction such impingement on my right to roam. Man is born free but everywhere he is being caught on camera and watched, prodded and poked by officious public bodies and taxed on the sly through a complex system of pedantic traffic codes and vindictive fines.

A dear and now old friend of mine in Madrid bemoans the day when in a newly democratic Spain it became illegal to perform a simple, sweeping U-turn in your car on the Gran Vía (think 5th Avenue in New York or Oxford Street in London). It symbolised to him the end of an age in Spain of joyful personal freedoms, of the time when you could smoke to your heart's extinction in cinemas, when you could park your car *"en doble fila"* (double line), when you could drive home at 7am after several *"copas demás"* (too many drinks) safe in the knowledge that the state would turn an avuncular blind eye. He misses the times when you could run with the bulls without inciting a Twitter storm of activist protest, when tapas were generous and good, when you could drink, dance and be merry all night and still have change from 1000 pesetas. He's fantasising, but not much. Ask anyone above the age of forty-five in this country about the Euro and what happened to the price of a coffee. They'll be happy to tell you.

Oh, go on then, I'll tell you.

For many years towards the end of the 20th century, coffee in a local bar cost 100 pesetas which was a little round coin that said *100* on it. The coin had a diameter of about three centimetres and was gold in colour. After the introduction of the Euro (cue a whistled rendition of *Ode to Joy*), a new coin went into circulation. It was about three centimetres in diameter, gold coloured and had a *1* on it. It seemed a good idea at the time to replace one coin with the other for everyday exchanges such as, for example, a coffee at your local bar. It was a seamless and practical transition.

It was only some time later that the nation realised that the price of that coffee had actually increased overnight from 100 pesetas to 166 pesetas. That was the exchange rate. Economists called it inflation. People across the country called it a scam.

But who cares? How many coffees can you drink in a week? Surely it can't make much difference? Correct. But it wasn't just coffee. The culturally venerated *"Menu del Día"* went from 1,000 pesetas to 10.00 Euros. Still a 1 and three 0s but with the decimal point in different places and one a full 66% more expensive. Guess which one. A cinema ticket at 600 pesetas became 6.00 Euros and a glass of wine shifted from 200 pesetas to 2.00 Euros.

This would have all been fine but soon people noticed, (people not being stupid), that their salaries did not benefit from this convenient rounding up. Funny that. Spain for many was never quite the same again.

Many years have gone by now. Memories fade, and since

then Spaniards have had plenty of metaphorical political and economic fish to fry, in addition to the just over 40kg per capita fish consumption per year that they physically fry, grill or bake. This is probably an unnecessary fishy tangent, but Spaniards will often tell you how they eat more fish than any other nation. According to my superficial research this is not true. That prize goes to Iceland, with the Maldives and Portugal apparently hot on their heels, or tail fins if you prefer. Truth shouldn't get in the way, however, of a good old-fashioned commonly held belief that informs cultural identity, not in this country or any other.

Meanwhile there have been as many political shifts to choke over as fish bones: the rise of a more extreme left and right, the push for Catalan independence, the exile of a former King for financial shenanigans and assorted acts of naughtiness, often nocturnal. All of these are big stories in themselves but, when you get right down to it, a lot can be traced back to the day when Carlos, my local bar owner, decided that, for convenience, one gold-coloured coin would be best replaced by another of similar proportions.

In or out?

I am still looking for a way out of Pamplona. Or a way in, actually. Or, at least, not to be stuck neither in nor out. It's time for affirmative action. I wind the window down and ask a passing shopper the way to the cathedral. Calling in all my years' experience as a free-floating global citizen, I'm banking that there has to be a car park underneath the main cathedral square and there has to be a hotel next to the cathedral and that hotel has to be nice doesn't it?

The passing shopper is matter of fact.

"Allí" (there), pointing with two raised eyebrows and a swift upward head nod in the direction of the end of the street. This is the most Spanish of gestures, simultaneously answering the geo-location question, while also letting you know what a prat you were for asking.

I look up and notice a large gothic structure. I get it. She is matter of fact for a reason. It is a cathedral and it is 60 metres away.

And there is a hotel next to the cathedral. I'm on a roll.

I've got my pen. I've got my notebook. I'm in Pamplona and I am about to tread where Hemingway trod. I'm also going to tread where I once trod. It was a long time ago and that me was quite different to this me, but it was me.

I came here once years ago during the *San Fermín* festival.

It was hot, crowded, drunken and I was with friends who afterwards all went different ways in life. But for those few days we were united in fever. It was not then the *"fiesta"* that Hemingway had known, largely because he had known it and spread the word. TV had arrived and with a global reputation comes colossal overcrowding.

But we spent a happy week sleeping on park benches, snatching hours of slumber here and there. We ate tuna from tins tipped onto long *"pistolas"* of bread. We went in the morning to watch the *"mozos"* run with the bulls. We drank cheap wine from cartons and bad whiskey mixed with Coca-Cola. This time around there'll be a lot less of a lot of those things and other things like the laughs. But there will be a bed with a pillow, and I reckon on first sight that the hotel looks like the kind of joint that may even stretch to a couple of fancily wrapped chocolates left on the bed and a complimentary bottle of water. Measured by quantity and quality of hotel trinkets, my life has moved forward nicely in these intervening years.

When I check in, the lady at reception gives me a map of the city accompanied by the robotic description she has delivered thousands of times before. As she speaks she marks each point on the map with an asterisk.

"Aquí está el hotel." (Here is the hotel.)

"Y aquí el Casco Antiguo y la Plaza de Castillo." (And here is the central Old Quarter and Plaza de Castillo.)

"Esta todo muy cerca, a unos cinco minutos andando." (It's all close by, about five minutes' walk.)

"Anda, lárgate ya…" (And now just sod off.)

OK. So the last one is not quite verbatim but looks can speak as well.

In an act of petty rebellion, I turn left out of the hotel instead of right as she instructed me. It takes me down a gloomy side street full of smelly bins on the arse-side of restaurant kitchens, before a heavily graffitied high brick wall indicates a dead-end street and I have to turn back. No need I think to highlight with my yellow pen the life lesson never learnt here.

The Plaza de Castillo is a vast and beautiful square in the centre of Pamplona, almost empty at this hour. Shoppers in the city centre have been and gone. Deliveries are being emptied from vans on all sides, global supply chains hemming us in, while an occasional tourist stares at the bandstand as if pondering a Miró.

"We had coffee at the Iruña looking out from the cool of the arcade at the big square," wrote Hemingway in the 1920s.

Sitting where he sat, I also order a coffee and look out from the cool of the arcade at the big square. The Café Iruña is a handsome old café and the cool arcade remains the same as it was 100 years ago, as does the square. It is easy to see why an American with a desire to drink and hang with friends would find himself sitting very comfortably in a place like this.

Me too.

But the second coffee is not as good as the first and the place is beginning to fill with others wishing to look out at the square from the cool of the arcade. Those others also wish to shout loudly about the relative merits and demerits of two supermarket chains. The debate is intense, fiery and committed. *Mercadona*, the Spanish national favourite, is cheaper but has limited choice while *Carrefour* is more expensive but offers more choice. This is as true as anything Hemingway ever wrote. He would have approved of the directness of speech and the honesty. But the muse has been interrupted and my fragile sense of time-travelling literary osmosis is gone.

After that I meander like the day. I remember that I have no place to go and no time to get there. I don't feel like lunch so I all-day graze, picking at *"pintxos"* whenever I feel hungry. To accompany there is good red wine always.

By the time I arrive in the cathedral cloisters I can feel myself trying to walk in circles in what is a perfect square. Lightheaded, I get back to the hotel and lie down on the bed.

Some time later, I wake up. It is neither night nor day. There must be something about this city that leads me to drink, sleep at odd times and walk around in wobbly circles. The wine this time is better and a hotel bed has replaced a park bench. I feel momentarily elated knowing that there is a reckless, youthful, eternal fun-seeker inside me still.

Maybe there will be some proper craziness ahead.

Or maybe not.

As that thought passes across my mind like an ocean liner on a distant horizon, I feel myself falling asleep again.

Loops

It's morning time again and it's time to leave. The impulse to move on is strongly reinforced by a confusing and expensive breakfast. This is a novice's error in Spain and I'm irritated with myself. There is always a decent bar just metres from wherever you are in a Spanish city and for not much money you can breakfast royally on toast with olive oil and tomato or Spanish omelette with good coffee, and it can all be done in minutes. Hotel breakfasts, however, are like feeding times at a zoo penguin pool but without the laughs and comedy capers. Grey-faced people queue up to pick unthinkingly over fruit, cheese, ham, eggs, pastries, cereals. They stand confused at assorted machines, like Neanderthals attending an early demonstration of round-wheel technology. The coffee machine presents 16 different options for coffee. It's not clear how to start the coffee-making process nor which size cup to choose from the stack, nor when the process has finished. That's a lot of nors for any human at this time of the morning.

Meanwhile, amidst all the choice of breads there is also the additional supra-gigantic technological challenge of getting the toaster to toast, not too little and not too much. This can often require one and a half loops through the hotel's conveyor-belt toasting machine and this is physically impossible. Loops can only be carried out in whole numbers. This means sticking a metal tong right in there before time to avoid burning the toast. That, though, is a poor trade off when you consider the new attendant risk of burning your knuckles on a red-hot orange element at over 520° Celsius.

And no. I am not exaggerating the temperature. I didn't believe it either but I'm a professional, and I would never mislead you on points of fact. Toasters really do reach those temperatures and higher. I could go on and explain more about the nickel and chromium alloy used to make the heating element of a toaster and how it was patented in 1906 and is more generally known as 'nichrome'. However, there really is nothing more dull than a bar-bore regurgitating newly-skimmed Wikipedia knowledge.

I want to get out of this place and it's not just because of the breakfast. The city is beautiful, the food and wine are beyond amazing, the buildings are imposing, culture and identity are strong and Hemingway literary trails are everywhere. I guess what I'm saying is that if you get the chance and you're in the 'hood you really should drop in.

But I've been in Spain a long time and Pamplona feels as uncomfortable to me as anywhere I've ever been. All countries have their own separate countries within their borders and this country feels far from my own Spain and my memories of the *"fiesta"* all those years ago so far off that they are now out of reach.

Back in the car I climb the ramp out of the car park and within minutes am on a main road out of town. Soon I've passed the flotsam of industrial estates and warehouses and am in open countryside. The morning mist is lifting to reveal green pastures and occasional houses with pitched roofs and beamed frontages. It has a Swiss air that issues an invitation to linger.

Today, though, is not the day. I'm heading west to a small town not far from Burgos.

Reading between the lines

When those letters from Carmen dropped through my London letter box they came always in the same style white envelope. Inside, one or two sheets of white A4 paper with neat, blue ink writing. Later on I learnt that Spanish schools placed strong emphasis on handwriting. Her writing was that standard, rounded, school-essay writing. It was neat and organised. So were her thoughts as far as I could tell. I couldn't speak, write or understand Spanish. I bought a little pocket-sized bi-lingual dictionary and laboured for hours deciphering meaning. It was the age of books. I examined the lines, between the lines and above the lines to detect texts, potential sub-text and motive. Was it lust or like? Amidst all of the impossible verbal conjugations was she expressing a previously suppressed desire to change her life and move to London?

Was she imagining a Hugh Grant London of imposing white villas with brightly coloured front doors, bookshops, riverside walks, kites on Blackheath and Chelsea galleries? Was she a dreamer too? Did I fit into the dream? And what if she were to find out that my London was not that London?

What if she knew that for my London you need to head a long way south to eternal high streets of betting shops, kebab joints, building societies, pubs with monster TV screens and menacing late-night tube stations. Keep going a bit further south and the Tube lines run out altogether and you are left with desolate far-flung suburban rail stations with adjacent, neon-lit, smoky, poky mini-cab offices picking up straggling late-night heavy drinking commuters who have lost their dignity somewhere on or around Victoria Station.

And her. My God. From a quiet town of tree-lined squares, washing hanging bucolically from balconies, easy café terraces and pure silence after lunch as the town sleeps its *"siesta."* I was imagining elderly gentlemen on bicycles with baguettes across the handlebars on their way to a neighbourhood bar for a vermouth in the shade, old ladies dressed in black sitting on park benches talking animatedly with children playing freely around them.

Why would she? Why should she? Was she also a hopeless, lost, unaware, immature romantic who was prepared to allow her life's path to be altered forever from a chance meeting one summer's night? Because I was. Or I thought I was. Sometimes at least.

Aside from hours studying that crisp, rounded handwriting I also wrote letters back, confronting head-on the demons of my very grave language impediments. All sentences I attempted had to be present tense. Spanish verbs were far too difficult for me to even contemplate a rumination on the past or projecting forward to the future. Being that present, let's call it turbo-charged mindfulness, may bring all kinds of benefits for wellbeing, but for a writer it's rather like trying to play a game of tennis all on your own locked inside a small wardrobe.

I determined to learn a small suite of verbs that could cover some key actions: to be, eat, drink, walk, sleep, work, like and to think. This would not make me Action Man but it would at least afford me the potential to sell myself as something other than plankton.

It's worth listing the verbs out so it's clear just what a profoundly boring experience it had to be for Carmen to read my letters. Boring, confusing and comical. 'To think' was in reality the only one that could identify me as a human rather than a frog. In my quest to impress, it seemed important, at least as an aspiration, to be able to share something that I thought.

I also lobbed three personal pronouns into my linguistic tool box: I, you, me and a smattering of nouns.

And then there was the stand-out shiny star outlier in my language-learning constellation. I had learnt from a guy in a bar (as you do) over a late-night rum and coke that adverbs in English ending in 'ly' could most times be translated into Spanish with the same word plus the ending '*mente*'.

For example:

- Automatically – *Automáticamente*
- Completely – *Completamente*
- Correctly – *Correctamente*
- Gently – *Suavemente*

OK. So that last one doesn't quite work as well.

- Happily – *Felizmente*

Neither does that one. But a 60–70% strike rate is not bad when you're desperate.

This new dog trick gave me a long-shot stab at a literary flourish which stood at least some chance of being right. That had to be better than no words at all.

So with this tool (match)box, I sat in the Duke's Head, a pub in my unglamorous corner of London, with a pint in front of me cobbling together letters to Carmen. My quest was to find that delicate equilibrium that would demonstrate literary flair, a complete, well-lived and cultured life, a special gift for learning languages, an enthusiasm for maintaining a relationship with her with, of course, a certain simultaneous aloofness to ensure that I would not be seen as (i) desperate (ii) lonely or (iii) psychopathic. I also wanted to convey a sense in which I was finding time to write as it was important, but that as I reached halfway down the second page I would have to stop, given my presence being urgently required at a theatrical first-night in the West End, a friend's book launch at the Barbican or a dinner date with a German heiress to a major engineering fortune.

Back in the day kids, we used to write letters using pens on paper and there was a standard form for saying that you were fed up with writing. It went like this: "I need to sign off now as..."

After "as" you could insert the lie that suited the occasion. In my case the truth was much simpler. I literally had nothing else I could possibly say. And then usually my friend Mark would turn up and join me at the pub.

"You're not still writing to that Spanish woman are you, you twat? Her mates must be pissing themselves laughing at you."

Mark had a lopsided leaning left brain. If lopsided sounds like a value judgement it's because it is, or at least it was at that time. He was studying Engineering and could not understand why I would be investing such large quantities of time fighting the immovable forces of real life that so clearly and exponentially outweighed any momentum I could muster from my weekly letters. Time proved him right and wrong.

But.

There is a but, which at the time I believed vindicated my extreme, unreasoning romanticism. Carmen kept on writing to me. It wasn't just a week or two or three. It was many months and over a year. It was the evidence I needed to continue to build my fantastical, beautiful and epic parallel universe.

And every letter that arrived had her sender's address on the back. A street, town, province and postcode.

What takes us anywhere?

So here I am 30 years later, on the road to a small town near Burgos. I would like to see the town that I once imagined, maybe the house where she authored the letters.

I am strangely and nervously exhilarated. The trip makes no sense, i.e. precisely the moment at which life usually gets interesting. I just have a wistful wish to touch an important point on my Spanish journey, to see if I can reconnect to that feeling, to the innocence, openness and absurdity of my younger self. Because I'm a grown-up now and no longer seek Hollywood endings or even Hollywood beginnings, the endings because they just don't happen, the beginnings because they promise more than life can ever deliver.

I know the scripts too well. I've read a lot and written a few myself.

In the movies, I would roll into town today, take a seat at a neighbourhood café and order a drink. The lady owner (guess who) would come over and we would exchange awkward, quizzical glances. After a number of false starts and a second glass of wine she would say my name. I would say hers. We would stumble over simple words and reach for the ends of sentences. We would sit and talk for hours. She'd show me around town. I would tell her all about my life, what happened next, how I came to learn the language properly, how

I learnt to conjugate verbs so I could talk about the present, past and future.

I could tell her that I love her country with its open spaces, hearty food, unfussy interpersonal relationships, outward simplicity and unspoken complexities. I could tell her that I have always been profoundly grateful to her, that I have never forgotten that night on the beach in Santander and that I have often wondered where she went and what she did.

Had I not met Carmen I never would have come to Spain. She was a pivotal figure in my life. That's why Mark down at the Duke's Head was both right and wrong.

But maybe those letters were half to Carmen and half to myself. Maybe the tortured verbs and linguistic contortion were ways of exploring another life and defining another me. It may be that I needed to find a new language. Or maybe this is low-grade, post-rationalising armchair psychology. For the definitive answer I probably need to get back down to the Duke's Head with Mark, get the beers and dry roasted peanuts in and talk it through as the two grown-up, sophisticated, urbane and consolidated members of polite society we nearly became.

The fact is that after that night on the beach, Carmen and I never saw each other again and after a year or two the letters definitively stopped. Just over a year after we met, I moved to Madrid, a classic, everyday tale of a guy in his twenties wanting a change, looking to get out of a job in London that had arrived too early. There was nothing extraordinary about that. I found a room in a flat in Madrid with a photographer who took more cocaine than pictures, but he was patient with my language skills. We would sit and watch daytime TV together. It's unorthodox but if you want to learn a foreign language you can do a lot worse than to immerse yourself in endless episodes of *Baywatch*. The situational context is always clear, the language is predictable and repetitive and the pictures give you big clues as to what is being discussed. This is an intended pun by the way in case you're not sure.

Just for clarity.

Meanwhile, however, the trail to Carmen ran cold. I have a very distant memory of speaking to her once on the phone. I think we may have said we'd meet one day. I think she may have said that she may be coming to Madrid and she'd let me know. I think I may have said that I was going to pass through Burgos. I actually don't remember. As all crime investigators will tell you, our memories are not reliable. Some memories in life stick, others don't. She didn't come to Madrid and I didn't go to Burgos. The letters had stopped, there were no more calls and we never met again.

And for now, it is extremely unlikely that Carmen would still be living in the same town. Spain's population shifts have been dramatic in the last few decades. There is hardly a day when politicians don't talk about the "*España vaciada*", the 'emptied Spain'. There are thousands of villages across the country clinging on for survival with tiny, ageing populations. In the second half of the 20th century, Spain's agricultural workers moved en masse to the big cities looking for work and a better life. By and large they found it and we now live in the age of the expanded, urban metropolis. Large cities offer work opportunities, universities, entertainment, transport connections and lots of the other serious stuff we appreciate in the 21st century. And most serious of all, they offer us permanent distraction. Cities are fun and when you're swiping left and right on Tinder the supply of dating options is almost infinite. Try swiping in parts of Castilla y León, the mightily sized province to the north of the capital and you may easily find yourself connecting with someone in a village 60 miles away. That's a long way to go for a quick one, or even a slow one or, in fact, any one.

Rural Spain has been left behind with many villages across

the country seeing their populations decline to literally zero. Some have a summer and holiday population surge as city-dwellers go back to their roots for a few days or weeks a year. When you talk to most Spaniards they will usually talk lovingly about their "*pueblo*". They will have often spent significant time there during school holidays and at weekends. They will have eaten Grandma's "*lentejas*" (lentils) there and they will still tell you that there are no better lentils to be had in the whole country. They will be proud of the "*chorizo*", wine, olive oil, cheese or ham or whatever is produced in their village and you will be encouraged to try some. Many Spaniards return for "*fiestas*", to see relatives and to reconnect with old friends. Some have to stay in touch because they own an old, crumbling family house which has to be maintained. After the death of a parent or grandparent it then has to be sold and the proceeds split, often at torturously slow speeds and acrimoniously as numerous "*hermanos*", (brothers and sisters) bicker about who gets what or, often, who pays what. Many of these old houses can be as much of a liability as an asset, requiring significant investment to get them up even to saleable standard and when the bills start rolling in, universal family love, peace and understanding can be tested.

But ties to the "*pueblo*" are weakening and in another generation or two the numbers of Spaniards with direct, meaningful connection to a "*pueblo*" will have plummeted. TV talk shows routinely air the options: hi-speed rural internet, remote working, investment in tech start-ups out of the main cities, eco-tourism, a potential upsurge in local production as the age of rampant globalisation stutters, a return to more labour-intensive organic farming. So far none of these have had a meaningful macro-level impact. But there is some hope. The global pandemic was perhaps a catalyst for a shift in our thinking. If we really want to cut back on our free and easy mucus sharing, we may just decide to up sticks and head for the wide-open spaces of these sparsely populated rural areas.

All of these factors stack up like a pile of poker chips against a chance encounter for Carmen and me today. If she has lived a typical life for a woman of her generation, she would have finished her university education and moved to Madrid, Barcelona or some other big city to work. She could well have moved to London or even New York. She may have completed an Erasmus programme in Amsterdam or Brussels and stayed there. Less likely, but possible, is that she stayed in Burgos, a provincial city of 175,000 people, big enough for reasonable professional opportunities and offering what people in these parts uniformly describe as *"calidad de vida"*, (quality of life). A weekend friends or family excursion to a small or medium-sized provincial Spanish city usually comes with a predictable and repetitive chorus of all and sundry, their mother and the accompanying golden retriever telling you that *"aquí en las provincias se vive muy bien."* (Here in the provinces you live very well). It's an unoriginal observation but like all clichés contains some truth. You may never have been to León, Zamora, Oviedo, Teruel or Cáceres but all of them and many more small and medium-sized cities across the country are wonderful places, and for visiting metropolis dwellers can seem for 48 hours like the definitive utopian sweet spot of beautiful old city centres, easy walking or biking commutes, sensibly priced housing, a splash of contemporary culture and decent local cuisine. Sunday night comes though and the motorways clog up as people return to the biggest smokes of all – Madrid, Barcelona, Valencia, Sevilla...

Whatever else she did or wherever she went, there is a high probability that Carmen has spent at least some time back in the small hometown over the years.

And there's another basic fact. I have one photo of her taken when she was, I guess, 23 or 24. I don't know if she has a photo of me but if she does it was taken when I was 27. I've taken it easy on the alcohol and been eating my spinach and chia seeds for years but despite my best efforts I am not physically unchanged by the passing of the last 30 years. I suspect she may be the same.

If we were to meet we would be absolute stone-cold strangers, unless perhaps I play the definitive identifying trump card of opening my mouth. A few distinctly Brit-accented verbs (even correctly configured ones) later, maybe, just maybe, she would have a dreamlike flashback to a beach under the night skies of Santander.

The short and winding road

The road is winding and the blue skies eternal. This is the land of vast cereal production, gargantuan open treeless fields and small hamlets. From time to time there is a petrol station, a roadside bar and an occasional tractor to slow me down. If Bruce Springsteen were Spanish this is the heartland that he would write about. He'd tell stories of a scorching sun in summer and biting cold in winter, of abandoned buildings where home fires used to burn, of families driven out by unemployment, of machines replacing people, of the arrogance of a disconnected globalised, city centric world, of economic injustice and migrating populations. He'd also be writing about love of the land and of neighbours and how people can resist.

Time passes happily and quickly, and soon I pass the sign at the entrance to the town. My heart is beating fast. I am breathing quicker. You could call it a kind of panic. What is the road that has brought me here all of these years later? Why?

I follow the sign to the *"Ayuntamiento"*, the town hall. In Spanish towns the *"Ayuntamiento"* is almost always located right in the middle on the main town square. It is usually a handsome building that looms large over the town and its population. This is not the time for a long philosophical essay on Spain's many layers of government and the overarching presence of Public Administration in daily life but I think it's a perfectly good time to share the gentle observation that *"Ayuntamientos"* almost always seem, to me at least, to be physically and spiritually oversized in relation to their towns and populations. They poke, pull, impinge and encroach on many minute aspects of daily life. It all starts with the flags. From the handsome building typically there will be several large flags hanging that sizewise would not look out of place on top of the Palace of Versailles or on Capitol Hill. There are often three flags: the national flag, the EU flag and the flag of the relevant autonomous region i.e. Andalucía, Castilla La Mancha, Castilla y León etc. There may also be a specific flag for the village with the local crest. That is, three or four everywhere except in Catalunya and the Basque region where local councils may very well give a wide berth to the Spanish national flag.

Where was I?

Oh yes. Flags, local councils and their central position in the life of small towns. Which is why I'm following the sign to the *"Ayuntamiento"* because I know that will lead me to the town centre and that there will be a square, probably a nice one, with a smattering of bars and terraces with their sunshades up, some local life and some well-planned tree cover for shade. And I know that I'll be able to get a drink to calm what now are nerves beyond anything I imagined possible when I had the idea to start this journey.

I park down a side street, walk 20 metres and there I am on the set of my own particular film, (see paragraph above for full description). It is not Romanesquely beautiful, nor monumental on the scale of a major city but this place is unassuming, pretty, well spaced and, in Spanish, *"desenfadado"*. I love this word. It literally means 'not angry' but it means something more like 'easy-going' or 'relaxed'. And yes, the town hall does have three large flags flying high over the population below.

It's late morning and the June sun is pushing the temperature dial up. It's too hot for a terrace so I head inside a bar on the corner of the square. It is dark inside and cool. The owner is shuffling fast from one end of the bar to the other, cutting slices of potato omelette, cracking open bottles of cold beer, pouring generous glasses of red wine and dispensing change to paying, departing customers on little plastic plates. In a world of hyper-inflation and a rising tax burden this particular entrepreneur is wisely running a cash only economy. I order a glass of red wine and with it comes an almost perfectly equilateral triangle of Manchego cheese and some bread. I sit with my back to the very loud TV and look out over the square. I feel like a man in need of a plan. Or maybe this is a plan in need of a man.

It's time to get practical and think this through. I open up my rucksack and one by one put my 'facts' on the table. I have three envelopes with Carmen's handwriting. They are stamped by the post office as being sent in Burgos on November 9th 1993, 3rd January 1994 and 29th April 1994. The 3rd January one is a long thin envelope containing a Christmas card which I guess she sent to arrive in time for "*Reyes*" (Three Kings) on January 6th which was then the main day for Christmas celebration in Spain. Since then there has been rapid encroachment on that tradition from the global phenomenon that is Father Christmas. "*Papa Noel*" has squeezed himself down the chimney of public consciousness into Spanish Christmases via Disney movies featuring elves and reindeer and a relentless supermarket musical onslaught of jingly-jangly Santa songs. This has generally buggered things up as we now have over-excited, over-sugared, present-grabbing kids acting weird twice over the Christmas holidays rather than once. All of that or she just forgot to send the card on time.

Of the other two envelopes, one is empty and the other contains five letters each with different dates spread over almost a year. I know that there were more letters than this but at some point they must have been thrown out or lost.

I also have a photo of Carmen. Well, actually, it's a group photo of Carmen with her friends from the holiday when we met. She is crouched in the front row, one of five. They are in front of a branch of a (still) well-known hairdressing chain. She is wearing a blue polo shirt and white shorts and has long brown hair. She looks happy. On the back she wrote, *To David, with love, Carmen*. On the Richter scale of love intensity it wasn't even a light breeze. She says *"con cariño"* which translated would be something like 'with affection' although that sounds a bit stuffily Jane Austen. Let's go for something in English like 'love' in the way that you write *love from Uncle Jack* in a Christmas card. What I'm trying to say is that our relationship was warm and friendly but not steamy and amorous.

By the way, and in case you're wondering, the Manchego cheese is excellent and combines quite superbly with the red wine as I scour my evidence.

Back to the samples.

Errrrr. That's it actually. I don't really have much more to go on.

The address is weird and I suspect problematic. It gives the name of a street indicating a group of *"chalets"* but without a house name or a house number. I checked it online and it didn't appear so I'm figuring I'll need some local knowledge. Maybe the street got renamed. Maybe it was knocked down. Maybe there are so few *"chalets"* here that everyone including the postman knows where they are and who lives in each one. I should briefly explain that *"chalets"* in Spain should not be confused with *"casas"* which is the generic name for 'house' that can be used to describe any kind of house. People will say *"me voy a casa"*, meaning 'I'm going home' but that doesn't tell you if they live in a flat, old house, new house, windmill, narrow boat or spaceship. *"Chalet"*, however, does mean a house, usually more recently built and considered generally to be nicer and more modern. So here in this small town there are probably only a few *"chalets"*, although there are clearly many *"casas"*. All of this exposition can be wearisome, I know, but I feel compelled to explain, otherwise things later won't make sense. And on the bright side you will now know next time you drive into a small Spanish town to head for the *"Ayuntamiento"* and also how to avoid any confusion between the multiple housing possibilities that exist on the Iberian peninsula. These are tiny slivers of marginal gain, but all learning is good learning, right?

And now comes, I think, the time to address the elephant in this storyline room. Google.

I'm guessing at some point it's crossed your mind that if all I want is to say hello to an old friend/flame/pen pal/love interest/fantasy then all I really need to do is google her name, check out Instagram/Facebook/LinkedIn etc. etc. ad infinitum and I'd find her. Come on, man, you know her age – more or less – her birthday, which university she studied at and you have an address. Surely that's enough. What's the matter with you? Why are you making such a big deal out of this?

Well, I have the answer. And it's not that I'm a tech luddite.

The answer is Spanish surnames. Carmen's surname is a surname shared by just under 900,000 Spaniards and she shares her first name with just under a million others. And if you think I'm making this up I respectfully refer you to Spain's National Institute for Statistics no less. They are big, official and they count these things.

It would all have been easier if I had ever known Carmen's second surname. The tradition is that people in Spain use their two surnames, their father's and their mother's, in that order. That means that on official paperwork someone may be called Miguel López Aparicio or Sandra González Callejo.

Having only one surname for a person in Spain is like walking into Starbucks and asking for a coffee. It's just not enough. They are going to want to know if that's a latte, Americano, espresso, decaf, skinny cappuccino or a roast pumpkin latte with caramelised goat's bollocks. 'Coffee' just doesn't do it. And neither does one surname in Spain if you want to find someone. Just so you know I did look on Facebook and, yes, I tried by city, by university and all of the cunning combinations I could think of but the numerical probabilities were stacked against me. There are hundreds of thousands of women all over Spain with the same name and surname to say nothing of the millions across the rest of the world. And I knew where she lived over 25 years ago. She could have moved a dozen times since then and may not even be in the country. And she may, like me, not share much on social media. And. That's a lot of ands and there are many more.

It was truthfully also a relief to realise that this was something in life that could not be resolved from the comfort of my sofa with a cushion on my lap and a laptop on my cushion. Finally there was something in life that could not be fixed by a click and a swipe. Or at least not by me.

Meanwhile, back in my new favourite bar the conversation has subsided. Some people have left to fix lunch at home. The owner is less frantic. It could be my moment to ask about the address as I stick down my 10-Euro note on the bar.

"Hi. I have a quick question. Do you know the *Chalets* Street? Ring any bells?"

Based on the face he pulls, my question could just as easily have been, 'Excuse me, mate, what's the square root of 364,543 multiplied by 12.5?'

"Never heard of it. It's here in this town?"

"Yes. Definitely."

(long pause)

"If they're chalets it has to be the chalets on the other side of the main road. That's all I can think of. Take a look up there. The chalets behind the supermarket."

"Carmen!" he shouts to his wife. "Have you heard of Chalets Street?"

"Never heard of it. It's probably the houses across the main road behind the supermarket," she answers back.

"Muchas gracias. Muy amable. No se preocupe..." And I walked out.

And yes, I did take a second shooting glance at Carmen, the bar owner's wife on my way out.

A prickly brush with authority

Back on the square I figure that the obvious thing to do is to go and take a look at these chalets, but I want some second and third opinions. So, before even I could possibly have imagined it, I cross the square to visit the town hall. I told you they are central to life in Spain. Someone there would surely know what was what with street names.

Remarkably, there is no queue and I go straight to the information desk.

"Good morning. Yes (very nervous cough). I'm visiting the town and I'm looking for the "*Calle de los Chalets*." Are you able to tell me where that may be as it doesn't appear on the street map."

"What for?"

Her reply startles me and I begin to feel the pressure. Her colleagues behind are listening in as well.

"Erm... I'm going to visit an old friend."

"What's their name? Maybe we know them."

Pressure turns to panic.

"Erm... well... I just wanted to find the street really."

I really don't feel like mentioning her name. She deserves privacy and who knows if one of those people listening knows her? What happens if one of those people IS her?

I'm not enjoying this conversation and I can see that she

sees me as shifty and suspicious. I feel that way, and probably look it too. It's time to search for my hero inside, for the lone man bravely standing up to the swinging axe and judgement of the state. I don't think it's the government's business, even friendly local government, to know why I want to know where a street is and who I'm going to see and I think that Carmen deserves anonymity too.

"Never mind... I'll take a walk and see if I can find it." I smile awkwardly.

"*No pasa nada. Gracias.*"

I leave a lot faster than I entered, ducking my head so I won't be picked up by the CCTV camera at the entrance. Call it survival instinct but I've watched those TV programmes where they show grainy black and white video footage announcing that 'this is the man that police would like to speak to', and I don't want to be that man.

I do understand of course. She's doing her job. A foreigner appears asking for a street name. He has come to see a 'friend'. He is carrying a rucksack containing she doesn't know what. His friend is not a sufficiently good friend for the friend to know where the other friend lives. He doesn't want to say who it is. We live in a time of stalkers, psychopaths, serial killers and terrorists. I am none of those. I come in peace, love and wistfulness, but all of that is hard to get across in a one-minute exchange at a local council information desk. The lady behind the desk does not want to get involved. If I were her, I wouldn't either.

I need to reappraise my approach. All that's needed is a cheery question asking directions without the back story, without raising suspicions, without looking and sounding like a weirdo. I can pull that off, I tell myself. Can't I?

I'm now walking towards the other side of the main road behind the supermarket to check it out. It seems like the best bet. On the way I get a cheery wave from the barber, who has stepped outside of his shop for a smoke. He has a friendly face and I also notice quite exceptional teeth. He must be in his 60s and I think they must be false. But they look good. His hair is simply cut and slicked back like Elvis in his prime, although a bit thinner on top.

"Excuse me. You wouldn't happen to know where the *"Calle de los Chalets"* is?"

"Never heard of it. But it's probably the houses on the other side of the main road behind the supermarket. What you should do, though, is ask at the post office. That's just over there."

"You're right. Good idea. Thanks…" And I walk off towards the post office. The barber has a point. If there's one place where they will know where letters get delivered it would be there.

Two minutes later I am inside the post office talking to a very friendly lady wearing a blue blouse and white neck scarf. She is relaxed, happy and keen to help. But she doesn't. The conversation repeats itself. She doesn't know either, compounded by the problem that she is new in the branch and lives in the next town along.

"And anyway. There are loads of letters delivered here because the postman knows the families, even without their address. But I can't ask him because he's not here. What you could do is ask at the bar next door. Paco has lived here all his life and knows everybody."

The bar next door really is the bar next door. Through that door Paco is behind the bar preparing some sandwiches for a group of construction workers. After a couple of minutes he finishes, delivers the foil-wrapped *"bocadillos"* across the bar and looks at me over a pair of headmasterly glasses.

My script is now slick and I believe I'm sounding more light and casual with every rendition.

"Hi. I'm looking for *"Calle de los Chalets."* Any idea where that is?"

"No idea. But it's probably the one on the other side of the main road…"

"Behind the supermarket?" I join in, just like you'd join in with the chorus of *Hey Jude* at a McCartney concert.

"That's it. I'd try there."

"*Muchas gracias.*"

I think that it's time to remove myself from this conversational loop and go and look across the main road behind the supermarket. Paco, by the way, also had a very fine set of false teeth. On my very limited population cross-section sample, this town may just have a higher per capita rate of perfect teeth than Beverly Hills. Maybe Carmen is a dentist.

I walk back to the car for the 400-metre drive. By the supermarket I take a right and there are some chalets, quite a lot of them. I'd say at least 100 or so. What I notice first is that all of the streets have names – proper ones. There is no "*Calle de los Chalets*" as far as I can see. The houses look like they were built in the 1980s. The timings work for my story and the consensus emerging from the town locals sounds plausible. It looks like the houses, when they were first built, were given that casual street name before more and more houses got built and someone in the town hall decided they needed proper streets with proper names. It's an interesting town-planning anecdote but it leaves my own particular trail running cold. The house I'm looking for could be any one of them.

Stepping out of the car I realise that my only option now is to walk up and down the streets looking at the name tags on the mailboxes. There you will have the names of the residents and there maybe, just maybe, I will come across the surname I'm looking for and perhaps even a second surname.

About half of the houses have name tags. Of those that do, some are too faint to be legible so I can't stroll nonchalantly by a few metres away. I have to stop at each one and ram my nose up against them. As far as I know there is no law against pedestrians zig-zagging up and down quiet residential streets nosing at mailboxes but I'm not enjoying it. It feels uncomfortable and intrusive and it's not why I came here. I came here to travel to another time and place, to see what I saw all those years ago in my imagination, to trace a very thin and gentle line back to my younger self and to indulge my appreciation for this wonderful country that I've called home. I'm not achieving that by acting like a snooping, crazy person. And I become aware of a man, sitting in his white van parked across the street, observing me. Probably not from the FBI, nor a mercenary marksman hastily hired by the not very friendly lady at the town hall, but I'm not enjoying being an actor in this little two-hander play. And I'm now properly hungry.

Back across the main road I stop for a beer, a plate of lentils and a brick-sized lump of bread to scoop up the sauce. It's delicious and I'm happy to take some time to savour it as I contemplate the impasse in my narrative.

I feel glad I came here to see this town. It's not how I imagined it all those years ago but it is exactly as I knew it would be today. In the meantime, I grew up and learnt the language and the culture that shapes it. It was the place where my Spanish journey began. Without those stuttering letters my life may well have taken a different course. I needed those contorted sentences and upside-down verbs to rearrange my thinking, to challenge myself to a less comfortable life. I needed the romance of impossibility. They were love letters of a sort.

Moments

Some hours later I stop the car on the side of the road. The June sun is high in the sky and now burning hot. I pull over in the perfect mother of all shades cast by an old, large, disused warehouse. With the car windows down the air cools. There is the faintest breeze and the road is quiet at this post-lunchtime hour. I want to wait a while for these feelings to pass: sadness, nostalgia, longing, sentimentality, exhilaration, feelings that exist beyond our capacity to explain, words inadequate.

Leaving this place is hard and so too is the thought that most likely I will never come here again.

Fuel for the journey

I am 20 minutes out of town and see that the fuel tank is running low.

I stop at a country petrol station with an air of the wild west. The attendant steps out from a small hut and grabs the pump. He's wearing an orange T-shirt and grey trousers.

"Up to the top please," I tell him and I circle back to the passenger side to get my wallet from my rucksack. Rummaging around the bottom I find it and pull it out to get ready to pay.

"65,00 Euros, please," he tells me.

I open my wallet to get the bank card.

"*Se te ha caido algo*," he says, (you've dropped something).

I bend down and pick up a little blank white card. I don't recognise it so flip it to see what's on the other side. It's a handwritten note:

'David... Una cosa más... escríbeme a esta dirección vale. Es la casa donde vivo con mis padres en Burgos... tus cartas me llegarán antes... un beso... Carmen...'

(David. One more thing... write to me at this address OK. It's the place I live with my parents in Burgos... I'll get your letters earlier... a kiss... Carmen.)

And then the name of a street, a street number and the number of the apartment. The address is Burgos, but this time the city centre. The writing is neat and the address is clear.

I have neither seen the card nor the address before. It must have fallen out from one of the letters. I cannot remember ever writing to her at this address and I don't remember her ever writing this address on the back of her envelopes.

I pay for the petrol and walk back to the car, physically shaking in a state between shock and elation. I suddenly have a brand-new piece of information. I have a proper address with a full street name, number, apartment floor and number. If this was a TV detective show there'd be an advertising break now. It's as close to a cliff hanger as I'm going to get.

I have an address for a house she lived in with her parents and I am 20 minutes' drive away. I check the address on my phone. Yes, it's a real street. It's on the map, I can see the street view and it is not a phantom housing development.

OK David.

Take it easy.

She probably doesn't live there now.

She will have moved away years ago.

It's been a very long time.

Etc.

Etc.

But.

But her parents may still be there. They would be in their 70s by now but it could just be. Families in Spain don't move house that much. The family "*piso*" (flat) may very well still be the family "*piso*." It is a definite possibility. Suddenly my mind is heating at the highest of its possible Gas Marks. Could today be the day when I meet her parents? What the hell would I say? Why would they let me in? They'll think I'm deranged or dangerous.

Could it really be that I am 20 minutes from standing face to face with Carmen? Do I have the guts to press the buzzer? What do I say?

When you hit proper adulthood it becomes rarer to feel

the pure, adrenalin-charged excitement of youthful first-time experience. We carry on having first-time experiences but root canal treatments and osteopath appointments don't belong in the same category.

For this short, delicious moment I am living on the edge, Ray Bans on, cruising fast as hell in my open top red Cadillac with white leather seats, music loud and pumping, on an open road with only desert to the side and mountains ahead.

Metaphorically.

I am actually moving along nicely at a steady 45 miles per hour behind a lorry, with my GPS doing the directional thinking for me again. My mind is free to wonder what if. And it is wondering. I'm sensorily overloaded.

The entry to Burgos is easy. It is off peak and there is very little traffic. The boulevards are wide as I come into the new part of the city. There are tall apartment blocks and wide avenues. These are areas that were designed on an architect's drawing board to house the wave of country-to-city migrants in the 1970s and 1980s. Spanish cities were built upwards not outwards. It's the Spain that tourists don't see much of. Tourists flock to city centres with their cobbled streets, cathedrals, Roman remains, old city gates and walls, museums, galleries, beautiful squares and fun nightlife. Think Córdoba, Sevilla, Madrid, Barcelona, Granada and many others. Burgos too has an imperious cathedral and charming old town with a riverside walk and busy streets.

But I've come to love the rites and rituals of these new-build areas. They represent in so many layered ways what I like about this country, and a lot of that liking is in the grit, grot and everyday. It's where real people live their lives and it's where you find out what people are like. As you leave the *"cascos antiguos"* (old quarters) of Spanish cities, the buildings get newer and uglier. There were a lot of bricks around in the '70s and '80s and they did pile them high and they did sell them cheap, really cheap, before the crazy housing and construction boom when house prices reached levels far beyond people's realistic ability to pay. That is also another story.

The visual aesthetic, of course, of the modern rings encircling Spanish cities cannot compete with the polished jewels of its centres: Granada's Alhambra, Madrid's El Prado and Barrio de las Letras or Córdoba's mezquita and old town. But there is charm and functionality in the building decisions and way of life that modern urban development encourages and largely imposes. People live in close proximity to each other. As neighbours squabble and bicker in their "*Comunidades*" (apartment block residents' associations) about who pays for the leaky roof or whether TV aerials should be renewed or whether the contract cleaners are doing a good job in the communal areas, it can seem that apartment living can be hellish. And it can be. There are some downsides and in the interests of balance I can tell you what some of them are.

If you're unlucky enough to have a window in your apartment backing onto the "*patio interior*", you will have to learn to live with the daily lunchtime clatter of pots and pans as people cook, the scratch of knives and forks on plates as they eat, and the lingering smell of fried fish after they have finished. If you're down at the bottom of the block, your natural light is going to be lousy.

These 'interior' apartments are in estate agent speak, "less sought after."

The apartment that no-one wants is the "*bajo interior*" (ground-floor interior). They are the herpes of the apartment world. "*Bajo interior*" means dark, cold and with a high risk of damp. There are even more negatives to ground-floor living. There's a good chance that down at the bottom of the block you will have to step out on to the interior patio and pick up knickers and bras that have fallen from the neighbours' washing lines above. And there is no real way of returning these flying clothing items that land like meteorites on your tiny patch of mother earth. Unless someone knocks on your door to reclaim them and they usually don't.

It's not socially comfortable to go door to door asking lady neighbours if they've lost their knickers. And, before I get cancelled, this is not casual sexism. I've lived in many apartment blocks and knickers and bras are dropped more often than tracksuit bottoms and T-shirts. They just tend to be the smallest, most fiddly items. And I speak with the weight of experience behind me. I've often been the fumbling dropper as well as the dropee. It's a common mistake easily made.

The washing lines people have on the higher floors often stretch from window to window so they are shared between neighbours. In order to hang washing out evenly using the middle of the line as well as the ends, without doing a trapeze-artist daredevil stunt, there is often a little pulley system. You pull the line towards you to hang each item and feed it out to push it away and hang the next. There is a moment when you are working the pulley, holding various items of clothing, often across a spare arm or between your teeth whilst simultaneously placing pegs on the line. You can see how complications arise. And this is just hanging the washing out. Later, you have to bring it in again. That's another tug on the pulley and more fiddling with pegs. You can see how things go wrong. And, yes, occasionally there can be overbooking situations with neighbours on the shared washing line, kind of like the moment when you arrive in a cinema with your ticket for F12 and someone is already sitting there. Tensions can arise as we humans revert to the cave people that we really are, defending our territory.

Even that is, when G14 could be a perfectly good alternative.

These washing-day roadblocks happen especially when your neighbour hangs out bedsheets. These occupy the entire washing line. On those days there is no alternative but to drape washing indoors like surrender flags from door handles, curtain rails and hangers, and use that crucial piece of apartment living kit, the foldable washing rack. If you do that and place the rack next to an open door or window the results can be very good and often, in fact, better as you get your washing back dry, almost as quickly, but without the not-so-faint, absorbed aroma of garlic prawns. That would be my considered advice. Up to you though.

But there's more. As a ground-floor-apartment dweller, as well as picking up assorted items of clothing from the patio, you may also have to get a broom out and sweep up prawn shells, sweetcorn, olive stones, toothpicks and little breadcrumb molehills along with occasional forks and teaspoons. After their lunches and dinners, unthinking and badly socially adjusted neighbours often shake out their tablecloths directly on to the interior patio. This shouldn't happen. It's a big no-no. Social convention is that you shake your tablecloth out onto your own kitchen floor and then sweep up the crumbs and put them in your bin. Most people do but some don't. Of course, they will never admit it. They hide behind the anonymity of being just one in the massed pile of apartments on the upper floors knowing they cannot be specifically identified and neither can their breadcrumbs. But the dark truth is there for all to see on the ground floors of interior patios across the country.

Apartment living also means that you see your neighbours coming in and out even when you don't want to and hear them snoring, farting and screaming at each other on the other side of walls that were built for physical separation, not acoustic isolation. You can call all of the above unwanted social contact and I can see that the case for a swift move to the countryside is building. However, I'm going to make the case now for the defence.

High-density housing forces people to live close to each

other and that makes for tolerance. Of course, we don't always feel tolerant but more human contact makes us more tolerant. We actually have no choice. We just have to put up with our neighbours. If we don't, within weeks we will end up in hospital with heart palpitations and/or chronic long-term indigestion.

Contrast that with people living in a detached house on the edge of town. Those people become like their house – detached. After a while they become irritated and suspicious of anyone even just walking past their garden and looking over the hedge.

Inside the name, design type, location and context of each of our housing typologies are large clues to their possible impact on social cohesion. It's not my job but is there an earnest postgraduate who'd like to develop this as a PhD thesis?

So, in a block of eight floors with six apartments on each, you're talking about nearly 50 apartments containing say an average of 3–4 people. That's 150–200 people living in a building with shared spaces. People meet in the lift and coming in and out of the main door. They meet at the shared swimming pools common in newer blocks. Their kids will tend to play with each other as it's easier for the parents to have kids playing safely nearby than lug them off to see a friend on the other side of town. They will empty their mailbox at the same time as a neighbour and grunt a good morning.

You don't have to be friends or get on especially well but it's better not to fall out with each other. Some do of course, with spectacular, hilarious consequences as whole families play out Chekhovian dramas across generations. But, on the whole, with everyone living in similar shaped and sized boxes and a majority following the unwritten codes of community living, it is easier for people to feel a sense of societal cohesion. It also makes a place feel more alive and more fun. Spaniards spend a lot of time *"en la calle"* (in the street). Street life is busier, it happens until late in the evening, massively late in summer but also in winter. Apartment living forces people out or they'd go crazy.

And then there's the miracle of services.

Step out the door in these areas and you will find everything you could possibly need to buy and consume in this and ten more lifetimes. Most street-facing ground floors are given over to shops and small service businesses. There are local supermarkets, banks, stationers, butchers, fruit & veg shops, bakeries, restaurants, bars, late-night convenience stores, chiropodists, dentists, beauty clinics, nail bars, hairdressers, psychologists, osteopaths.

You need it? You've got it.

You don't need it? You've also got it.

High-density housing brings business because businesses need footfall. This means that the punters have everything on their doorstep.

And hidden from view inside most apartment blocks are the legions of micro-sized companies of lawyers, accountants, property managers, public notaries and – my favourite of all – *"gestorías"*. *"Gestorías"* are usually also accountants but they offer everyday administrative services: renewing passports or national ID cards and dealing with Social Security and an exploding kaleidoscope of government departments. Back in the day these *"gestorías"* were pretty essential to navigate an overblown and labyrinthine Spanish state. The alternative to paying a *"gestoría"* was booking your annual holiday leave to get in the queue for a few days, (expressed on a net cumulative basis), at a ticket office window at some ugly, monolithic building for whatever mundane, pedestrian and pointless *"gestion"* was demanded of you. There were myriad demands placed on the poor average citizen as the state sought to justify itself, tinkering and twiddling with every hidden corner of our little lives. And each form was requested in duplicate and triplicate and then stamped in another office on the other side of town, another office to which you would have to go personally. It's got better but *"gestorías"* still make a good living and people still know that when you go to any office of any of the long arms of the state, it's a good idea to take your birth and marriage certificate, driving licence, national ID card, national health card, tax identity form, a copy of a recent utility bill showing your name and address, a recent bank statement, the deeds to your house, any rental contracts and a hard paper copy of each of those things, just in case – *"por si acaso"*. That's for starters. Beyond that, a large sandwich, some water and a hip flask of whisky are good ideas. With all of that, you have a chance.

I have come to love the Spanish word *"gestion"*. Translated to English it would be something like 'errand' or 'small administrative matter'. Brits or Americans would say 'I have some errands to run', or 'I need to tie up some loose ends' but these don't get anywhere close to communicating the depth, complexity and significance of the Spanish version. People in Spain talk regularly about *"gestiones"*.

"Tengo que hacer unas gestiones" (I have some *"gestiones"* to do) is a coverall sentence that people can use in multiple contexts. The *"gestiones"* themselves can cover thousands of small everyday tasks that need taking care of: renewing a driving licence, a new photo for an ID card, paying a bill, signing a form at the local notary's office, closing a bank account, doing a car service, filling in a tax return, dropping by an apartment you have rented out to check all is well. It's all good stuff that needs to be done.

Modern public services have improved and much of it can be done online. But not all of it and the cultural significance of the *"gestion"* remains.

The *"gestion"* is an elegant way of saying that people have stuff to do that doesn't involve you. It may be that a clandestine hour is needed to sleep with a neighbours' husband or wife or to have a couple of extra beers on the way home to postpone having to see your kids. It can often be an excuse for lateness. "I had some *gestiones*" people will say as they arrive 45 minutes late for an evening drink. People will tend not to ask what those "*gestiones*" are. It's just better not to ask. I love the fact that this code is understood. It is a person's right to privacy and to some secrets. If you don't ask me questions, I'm not forced to lie. Spaniards generally don't like being questioned.

"*¿A ti que te importa?*" (what's it got to do with you?) they will ask if you tread unwittingly across or into someone's privacy-protecting moat. And soon after that the drawbridge will be raised.

"*¿Por?*" is also a standard response to a question perceived as too personal. Literally this means 'Why do you ask?' Less literally, it means, 'Sod off. What's it got to do with you?'

The "*¿por?*" question will come with a 45-degree swivel of the head, a furrowing of the brow and swift, direct eye contact. Is the ape in you sensing the body language signals?

I've now parked the car in the street written in blue ink on the little white card. It feels familiar, like so many other streets I have been to all across this country. The recycling containers are banked up on one side, blue for paper, yellow for plastics, green for general rubbish. There is a gym, a bar and a sports physio clinic. The street is neat, clean and modern.

At street level there is the large office of a transport company and then comes the entrance to Carmen's apartment block. It has an impressive new steel and glass door with big funky signage announcing the address. There is no confusion about where I am nor any need to ask around. I look up and see a high rise nine or ten floor pink brick block. It must date from the late 1970s or early 1980s. At the end of the street is a main avenue with triple traffic lanes on either side and young trees planted symmetrically down the middle. Opposite the apartments is a bar with its sunshades up and a busy terrace. The newly installed ground-floor entrance gives the block a solidity and sense of quality that the building itself doesn't really warrant. But it looks good. Through the glass I can see shiny marble floors, a staircase and a lift with a brushed aluminium door. Some money has been spent on this recently; there's a new set of mailboxes installed on the wall in brilliant, polished beechwood. All of the individual mailboxes have the names of the apartment owners neatly written on them. I'm now peering through the glass, covering my eyes to block out the light. The names are too far away to be legible. I'm looking suspicious again.

I just need to wait for someone to come along and open the door and I'll walk in. First, I want to check the mailbox name. I say first. That may very well be first and last. If the name on the mailbox doesn't match the surname then I reckon I'm done. Amongst my heart palpitations and cold sweats driving to Burgos I did actually think, and I decided that I want to keep weirdness and legally actionable erratic behaviour in a public highway to the absolute minimum.

But here I am, hanging around outside an apartment block on the outskirts of a northern provincial Spanish city waiting for someone to open the door so I can casually slip in. With smartphones there is no longer any need to just loiter on street corners. I bury my head in my phone and look busy.

After just a few minutes, a grey-haired resident comes along the street carrying some shopping bags. He puts a bag down to get his key out. After a bit of fumbling he opens the door.

"Can I help you with the bags?" I say.

"*Gracias…*"

I pick up his leftover shopping bag and take it inside to the lift. He calls the lift and when the door pings open I put it inside for him.

"*Muy amable. Gracias,*" (very kind of you) he says.

"*No hay de que*," (not at all) I reply.

The lift door closes and I wait a couple of seconds to make sure that he's on his way up and that I don't have an audience. I'm in and it was easy.

The mailboxes form a long rectangle, four boxes high and around eight boxes long or maybe ten. All I need to do is to look for 5B. I scan the rows of boxes. First floor, second floor, third floor, fourth floor.....

They all have neatly written names, first names plus two surnames: *David García Tarancón, Patricia López Mayal, Ramón Gallardo Pérez, Pilar Muñoz Pastor...*

I get to 5B. Nothing.

'Nada'.

There's no card and there's no address.

And there's nothing on the little wooden door apart from a small glue stain where the address card used to be. It is definitely the 5B box. It's clearly marked but the only mailbox with no owner. Inside the mailbox I can see a pile of envelopes and leaflets, the mounted-up mail that you find at an unoccupied apartment. On top of the pile I can see a flyer advertising a two-for-one pizza deal.

It's not the deal I was hoping for.

The lobby is quiet and I am on my own. Inside these four walls it feels like there's not much I can do. I will never be back again so I figure I may as well try just one more thing.

I step outside onto the street and press the buzzer for 5B. No reply.

Next I buzz up to 5A. Maybe a friendly neighbour would have a memory or a forwarding address? No reply.

5C. These are all the neighbours on the same floor. If anyone here were to have known her or her family it would be them.

There is no reply.

I step down onto the pavement outside and take a last look

at the front of the building. It was here that my letters criss-crossed with hers all those years ago. It was here that she came walking back from university. It was from this door that she would leave in the morning carrying a white envelope to post to a near stranger in London.

One day, some years ago, she left this place for ever and I sense now that I will never know where she went. She moved on as I did, as we all do. Maybe she's thought about me once or twice over these years, like I have of her. Maybe she wondered what happened to me. Maybe she visited London and wondered which streets I walked.

It matters and it doesn't matter at all, just another whispering moment in this beautiful, intense, fragile and so very transient life that we are all living. Things just end and we move on. We have all been to many places.

Heading East

Some hours later and I am back in the car heading south and east on the trail of Cela. I was in my 20s when I picked up an English language copy of his *Journey to the Alcarria* in a secondhand bookshop on the Charing Cross Road. I was doing some lunchtime browsing around the corner from the ad agency where I worked on Cambridge Circus. I felt returning after lunch occasionally with a couple of obscure novels was good for my personal brand positioning as a thoughtful, sensitive creative copywriter who could very well be a sound dating option for our front-of-house receptionist. That construct didn't work with her but I did buy a few books and I even read some of them.

I bought the book because I liked the front cover. That is exactly how I judge books. How else are we supposed to judge books? OK, so there's the blurb on the back cover but most books are considered a 'literary tour de force' or 'astonishing' by someone.

The cover had a purple border and in the middle an evocative photograph of two goats, one white, one black, who appear to be staring each other down, and in the background, a lady sweeping the street. I liked the fact that it was thin. Thin books are easy on the eye, fit comfortably into pockets and, by volume anyway, demand modest time, intellectual and emotional investment to read. After a period in my 20s of earnestly reading/scanning a lot of serious heavyweight literature, measured by both content and kilos, I also started to observe that many writers have something to say and that 'thing' could be said with fewer words.

Poets do it, chiselling and chipping at their work like sculptors until they find the perfect shape and reduction in form. It is the literary polar opposite to the books as 'plates of cabbage' model I was brought up with. Books had to be read from cover to cover even if they were turgid, incomprehensible or just overly long.

"It's good for you so you'd better get to the end."

There is truth in this but the joy of adulthood is that we can discover parallel and alternative truths. I discovered it can also be a sweet release to abandon a book because it's dull or impenetrable. I think I developed a healthier reader/author relationship. Yes, it's my job as a reader to make time to read but it's also the author's job to encourage me. That's fair, isn't it?

Apart from being light, easy to carry and with an attractive front cover, Cela's book was a pleasure to read. It is observant, poetic, human and direct. I discovered him to be a master of rhythm and pace and the affectionate observation of people. Reading Cela at that time seemed to me to be better than any number of workshops, masterclasses, bubbles, huddles or weekend writers' retreats in the country. And this was all with the English translation. I could only imagine then what the original Spanish version would be like. Some years later I was able to discover that too and it was even better.

The basic premise of the book could not be simpler: one day Cela leaves his house in central Madrid to go on a trip to the Alcarria. He has no fixed schedule, route map nor plan. He simply goes exploring. This elemental idea appealed to me beyond that of perhaps any book that I have ever read and I have carried it with me ever since.

It is now late and I am beginning to feel tired. The GPS tells me there are 2 hours 14 minutes left to Guadalajara and I'm going quite a way beyond there. A much better plan is a glass of wine, a comfy bed and some sleep.

I'm in luck. The next roadside petrol station also has a cafeteria and small hostel. My expectations are pitched low for the accommodation, and opening the door to the room, expectations are fully met. There is a single steel-framed bed, a plywood bedside table and some red drapes. The view is over the car park and main road beyond. The room has a tiny bathroom with a shower jammed in the corner. But the door to the room shuts with a satisfying clunk and even has a functioning lock. It's not a place made for lingering but I'm not going to. I leave my bag in the room, lock the door behind me and head downstairs for a glass of wine.

Less than 30 minutes later I'm back upstairs. I set the alarm for 6am and fall asleep.

The morning after

In the morning I pass the time in the car listening to the news. On this journey I have placed myself by choice in an unworldly parenthesis, leaving behind just for a while so much of my day-to-day and the pokes, prods and jabbering of constant communication.

Today even the news sounds timeless. The political scandals, distant wars and stock market turbulence could be news from any day in the last 50 years. Being in temporary suspension outside of the news feed and from my newly acquired distance it all seems to be about fear. The questions are the same. What does this mean? Where does this leave us? What is the future going to look like? For this time, at least, I'd prefer not to care.

East of Guadalajara, the landscape is familiar to me and comforting. I have passed through here many times on day trips and short breaks. Weekenders from Madrid tend to head north or west to the mountains of Guadarrama or Gredos or even further to Valencia, Alicante or the southern coasts. That partly explains for me the miracle of the Alcarria: its proximity to Madrid, a city of 6 million, counting the whole Madrid region not just the city and yet its wide-open feeling of space.

I grew up in London, rammed into England's southeast corner, a place where it is difficult to ever feel you are away from people. Mainly, because you're not. You need to head a long way north or west before experiencing any sense of wilderness. The towns and villages just keep on coming while roads and railways criss-cross the landscape like a pastry lattice on a treacle tart. You could head south or east but that would leave you floating in the cold, oily waters of the English Channel, – a wilderness of sorts I suppose.

The Alcarria has none of the drama of the Picos de Europa in Asturias or the desert dry starkness of Almeria. It is gently rolling agricultural land. Yellow fielded crops take on summer luminosity when the sun shines bright. The soil is red, you can walk in vast lavender fields in July just before they are harvested and everywhere there are pots of honey for sale.

For a writer with a romantic myopic selection bias or even a humble copywriter knocking out copy for a tourism website it would be easy to describe the region as 'unchanged by history'. This would be banal and false. As well as pretty medieval villages and rustic agricultural landscapes there are also wind farms, a major motorway cutting through on its way to Zaragoza and eventually Barcelona, universal internet access and even a high-speed rail link connecting to Madrid to the west and Barcelona eastwards. Around one of the high-speed rail stations is a newly built city that was envisioned and built in the 1990s and early 2000s, promising a utopia of parks, wide pavements, bicycle lanes, gardens, schools, supermarkets and spacious modern family housing, all with fast access to central Madrid and just a few minutes from Guadalajara, which as a city of nearly 100,000 people offers all the stuff that most of us need or want. And all of this with house prices significantly lower than in Madrid or its more immediate suburbs and dormitory towns.

It's a winning combination, right? And yes, it looked and sounded amazing on paper and even better in the slick videos and 3D architectural models. And here, dear reader, I need to come clean about those three words 'amazing on paper'. For it was I, who, as a humble advertising agency copywriter, was charged with writing a lot of the blurbs describing this new Jerusalem for glossy brochures and the website. I remember very well a couple of meetings with some sharp-suited executives from the principal construction company and promoter and one meeting with the very big boss. He was ambitious and exuded confidence, both deeply necessary qualities if you are planning to build 10,000 new homes for a brand-new population of 30,000 people and also to sell those homes based only on floor plans and before the train station is built.

He talked and I listened, noting his key points in my creative's Moleskine notebook (as favoured by Hemingway), jotting down 'quality of life', 'open spaces', 'easy access', 'fresh air'. As well as jotting these points down, I made sure he could see me doing so, circling particularly vital messages flamboyantly with my 'key point' red pen so he could feel confident that the little people like me had understood the big idea. Copy is more likely to be signed off later in the approval process if the punters feel like they've been listened to at the briefing stage. Doctors also know the therapeutic value of allowing patients to articulate the problem of their creaking knee before routinely prescribing a bit of rest and paracetamol to alleviate the pain. And there was no clever word play intended with the word 'articulate', but even after tortuous rewrites and editing, I've decided to leave it in, even knowing that it is a comedic error to oversignal a joke. But life in the end is a series of decisions, close calls, near misses and finely balanced editorial decisions, don't you agree?

Apart from meeting the key protagonists I also paid a visit to the site itself. At that time, around 20 years ago, it was a massive, flat open space with dozens of flags fluttering in the breeze displaying the construction company's logo. Measured by flags, the construction company had certainly arrived and no-one could be unclear about the scale of their ambition. There were already wide avenues laid out in Roman-style straight lines with neatly planted sapling trees and foundations being laid for the first of the apartment blocks and chalets. All that was needed was for the diggers to keep digging, the cranes to keep on swinging and the money to keep on flowing.

You've guessed it. That didn't happen.

The construction boom turned to bust. Supply had massively outstripped demand. There were far too many houses for sale at exorbitant prices with banks no longer prepared to offer mortgages.

Economists called it a credit squeeze and the bursting of the housing bubble. Everyone else called it a monumental balls-up. Houses were left half-built, entire pavemented streets leading absolutely nowhere were left abandoned, while promised vital services like schools and shopping centres were canned. The circle was truly vicious especially for people who had bought in early.

Without inhabitants there was no demand or justification for essential services and without those services it was impossible to attract people to come and live.

For more than just a few years Spanish construction companies had forgotten that as well as building houses, you have to sell them, and to sell them you need people, i.e. fundamental population data and demographics need to be moving in the right direction and finance needs to be available to those who want to buy the houses. Someone hadn't noticed that there were some pretty wacky shapes to those supply and demand curves around then.

Now it's at this point usually where we all snigger and say 'I told you so'. The media has had a lot of fun with all of this. It is a Spanish newspaper, TV and clickbait staple: the tale of the airports built and never used, the toll roads built for billions that see no traffic, the tens of thousands of houses across the country left unsold and unoccupied. And, yes, there have been plenty of jaw-dropping stories of ego, hubris, self-aggrandisement, corruption and general stupidity. But we humans, we're really good at being smart after the event. We do hindsight a lot better than foresight.

And here I'm prepared to put my head in the stocks and have some rotten tomatoes lobbed at me, – only soft ones please. Back in the day I sat silently through the meetings, made my notes, wrote the copy and took the pay cheque. I wasn't even a scraggy minnow in the overall ecosystem, but I was there, along with the much bigger fish, all of whom eventually got fried. And those fish were numerous.

The banks put up the money, the local councils gave permission to build and the average punter did their sums and concluded that there was no potential problem in having a mortgage of five, six or seven times their income. It was a very large game of human domino dumbness. Each domino knocked over by the previous one until there really was no last man standing.

*Note to self: Develop Human Domino Dumbness (HDD) as possible TV game show or full body size Christmas party game.

So roughly 20 years later here I am on the road to the Alcarria and the infamous development is literally a few metres off the road that will take me there. It's definitely time for a quick stop-off to see how it's all going.

At the entrance is a very large roundabout with, as its centrepiece, a towering sign inspired spiritually and physically, I suspect, by the famous 'Hollywood' sign.

CIUDAD VALDELUZ.

After the headline comes more modest content, a series of red brick apartment blocks and rows of modern houses. The apartment blocks offer no visual surprises. They are of their time. Function wins by a huge margin over form but once inside they will be modern and probably have balconies, terraces and swimming pools in the communal areas. They are no better or worse than a million other apartment blocks across the country. The trees have grown in the last 20 years and cast decent shade across wide tricycle-friendly pavements. There is a very American suburban feel to this place. The park is highly landscaped, well maintained and comes complete with a pond which comes complete with ducks. There are even signs warning drivers to slow down for ducks crossing the road – a very cutesy touch.

If those ducks crossing the road were to be on their way to the town centre, however, they may have a long and unrewarding walk. There is no town centre as such, not in the way of lively main squares or buzzy high streets. In one area there is a little sprinkle of cafés, a small supermarket and two or three neighbourhood shops, enough for everyday living, assuming you are happy for that everyday living to take place within a rather limited frame. It reminds me a bit of a cheaply made Australian soap opera where the same cast of actors and extras shuffle endlessly backwards and forwards between a very small number of locations.

The lady at the bar has the same kind of glasses as Velma from *Scooby Doo* and a mighty collection of silver jewellery on her wrists reaching halfway up her arm. She has a very cheery smile, the coffee is excellent and sitting on her terrace in the shade I enjoy watching the small snatches and polaroids of everyday life.

The population stands now at around 4,000. It's a very long way from the originally planned number of 30,000 but it is increasing slowly year on year and there are enough people now for the place to actually count as a place and not a ghost town.

And there are reasons for optimism. Several high-speed trains still pass through every day, offering 25-minute connections to and from central Madrid and just 2 hours 40 minutes to a distant Barcelona should you fancy a Gaudí fix. It's just a few minutes from Guadalajara for shops, cinemas, restaurants and injections of culture, there's some very pretty countryside close by and house prices remain low. I'm not an expert and, as we've learnt over the years, it is not clear who is, but I reckon that this is a very slow burner. It will never become that bold, original vision but it may just find its place in the world and its sweet spot in the housing market. That would be good news for residents and good news for the boss of the now-bankrupt construction company who could have his very sweet and definitive 'I told you so', moment, even though he may have to live until he is 150 years old to see it.

I am now back in the car and heading east. If Cela had been travelling today I think, given the same choice, he too would be heading towards Pastrana.

Encounters in Pastrana

It is mid-morning when I arrive in Pastrana, the perfect time. The sun is bright but still not high in the sky. The streets are cool and shady. It's the time of day when people go about their business before the intense heat of the afternoon sun drives them back indoors. I park in a street just off the *Plaza de la Hora*. There is a plaque upon entering the square commemorating the visit of Cela on the days June 13/14/15, 1946 with an inscription transcribed from his book: *the first sense that the writer had was that of finding himself in a large medieval city, a grand medieval city*.

He describes it perfectly. But it is clearly not a city in today's terms.

Pastrana's population according to the local council website is 850, a population which has been in recent year-on-year decline. In 1946 it was closer to 3,000. The population of Spain in 1946 was approximately 27 million. It is now 47 million. Without reaching for calculators we can see that we have two numbers heading in polar opposite directions, a growing national population and a declining town population. Our only conclusion from all of this is that the town has lost relative weight. That, however, doesn't change the total and absolute veracity of Cela's description and there is no better place to start than in the *Plaza de la Hora*.

The square is dominated by the *Palacio Ducal* which at the time of Cela's visit was derelict but is now restored. To the left and right stand rows of medieval wooden-beamed houses with an open fourth side offering uninterrupted views over a valley given over to small-scale agriculture.

I am anxious to walk in his footsteps, to see what he saw and to see how it has changed. First, I find a quiet corner in a small bar so I can read his chapter on Pastrana again. His prose is brilliant, immediate and unfussy, full of poetry with not even a pinch of mawkishness. And underneath his fearlessness as a writer is palpable human compassion.

He writes extensively of his encounter with Don Mónico Fernandez Toledano (Don Mónico) and Don Francisco Cortijo Ayuso, (Don Paco). Don Mónico is the mayor and Don Paco his deputy. The three men share vermouth, olives and conversation. His hosts are proud of their town and show hospitality far beyond formality. On the second day Don Paco offers Cela a car journey to nearby Zorita de los Canes before returning after nightfall to Pastrana for drinks at the casino. The respect and pleasure in their conversation is present in the text. Cela was enjoying himself. It was a time when visitors came rarely and they were treated like guests not as a source of revenue.

After this late-night encounter the book ends – without final thoughts or neat summaries. His journey ends as it began. One day he left to travel and then some days later when the time was right, he returned home. Writers can struggle to end a story. It is tempting to seek conclusions and resolution, to tie up the loose ends. But life is a long series of loose ends and they can't always be tied up. And life one day stops.

And here I am wondering whether Don Mónico and Don Paco have family left in Pastrana. Did they remain here? Did they have children? Are those children still here?

Returning to the main square, I stand a while and inspect

more closely. I am seeing what he saw. The only intrusion from the 21st century is the cars parked around three sides of the square. It is not pretty for the occasional visitor but cities, even medieval ones, cannot be preserved in aspic. Residents have needs and rights and require a place to leave their cars. Beyond that it is practically as Cela would have seen it.

Walking up the main street there are a few small bars and shops. There is animated conversation in doorways and between neighbours who pass each other with green plastic shopping bags, coming to and from the butcher, bakery and grocery. There is a light feeling in the air. Perhaps I am projecting myself onto the world around me seeing it not as it is, but rather how I am. I see a place at peace with itself on a scale that is human and liveable.

This positive energy takes me walking a few hundred metres to the town hall. There is a council worker at the information desk, in a protracted conversation about her payslip and whether next month she will recoup the money she wasn't paid this month. She is wearing steel toecap boots, blue council-issue trousers with fluorescent yellow strips on the borders for nighttime visibility and a matching blue polo shirt. Her dark hair is pulled back in a ponytail, her face open and friendly. The man behind the desk speaks quietly and empathetically. He is definitely on her side. He could choose to be officious and awkward, but he isn't. He is on her side and after some minutes of explanation and negotiation the position is clarified and she leaves happy, wishing me a good day on her way out.

I take my turn.

"Hi. I'm passing through looking around a little bit and I was wondering whether, as the town hall, you may know anything about the mayor or the deputy mayor at the time of Cela's *Viaje a la Alcarria*...

"It's just out of interest. Are there family of his left here in Pastrana?"

Maybe I'm not the first person to pass through asking the same question but the man is immediately open and communicative.

"You mean the mayor? Mónico? Or the deputy Paco? No. Both of them died years ago and neither had children so there's no family left."

"I guess it would be unlikely..." I say. "It's been a long time."

"Yes. But there's a house for sale just off the *Plaza de la Hora* on the main street, above the grocer's. It's on the left as you go down. You can't miss it. That was Don Paco's house and they're selling it. I think it's his family selling, maybe nephews. I'm not sure. You could call the number."

Is this the thrill that the Watergate journalists Bernstein and Woodward felt when they met secretly with Deep Throat and received some new piece of information on an embattled President? Could I really be on the threshold of making a real human connection to that moment in 1946 when those men came together here in this place? On my small scale and completely absorbed in this story it is a major breakthrough. I'll follow up but first I want to walk a bit more.

I say my thank you's and leave the building. Just around the corner is a much smaller square, *La Plaza de los Caños*. At one end is a fountain in the form of a goblet.

I take a seat for a while on a bench in the shade and play a little game of spot the difference. What could have changed since 1946? It is a well-proportioned square with pretty old buildings on every side. There is a small hotel in one corner. In the opposite corner there is a medieval building, with beams supporting the roof, that has been refurbished with a new façade. It is not a total triumph of architectonic integration but it definitely could have been worse. The colour of the stone sits comfortably with the other buildings. Outside, the doorman is sweeping the steps and talking to two men sitting on another bench. They sit close to five steel bins where residents bring down their rubbish, a small 21st-century testimony to the disproportion of our excessive consumption.

The square has a wonderful acoustic. Quiet conversations reverberate off buildings. It combines with the treble clef of birdsong from the trees above and distant dog barks. A trades-man comes walking by talking on his mobile, explaining the repair needed on a malfunctioning washing machine.

Filmmakers could easily spend hundreds of thousands of dollars attempting to recreate this soundscape and set. It is a theatrical stage on which we are all temporarily players and I am included in the scene, notebook in hand.

After some time, the church bells ring to break what had become almost total silence.

A phone call

The man in the town hall is right. The sale sign is easy to find directly over a small grocery store heading back to the main square. I take a photo of the number. It's a regular mobile number and could very easily be an estate agent. The temperature is rising now and I look for a bench back in the *Plaza de la Hora* to make my phone call. There is a stone bench free under a thickly leaved tree.

I dial the number... 6-0-9...

After a couple of rings there is a female voice.

"*¿Si? Diga.*"

I explain who I am, where I am and why I am calling. I explain that I am not interested in the house as a potential buyer. I explain that I have visited the town hall and that I am writing a book. I try not to babble.

After a minute, there is a moment of silence and the lady who has a naturally warm voice and an immediate aura of trust begins to talk.

Of course, she can help me and tell me whatever she knows and she's happy to answer questions. Yes... Don Paco was her uncle. He died in 1992. He had no children and so after many years it is the family's job to sell the house. There is no-one left in Pastrana and no need for the house. He was a doctor and she confirms that the day he met Cela for the first time in 1946 was exactly as he describes it in the book. But the encounter did not end there. The two men became friends and that friendship lasted a lifetime. Don Paco's wife also became friends with Cela's wife.

I sit listening to her stories just yards from where this first meeting took place. Is this how rock groupies feel when they get within touching distance of their idol?

"Is it OK if I make a few notes as we talk?" I ask.

"Sure. No problem."

She tells me that the house is for sale, now completely emptied of her uncle's many thousands of books. It is very large and needs modernisation.

The friendship between the two men lasted a lifetime and when Cela returned from Sweden in 1989 with the Nobel Prize for Literature, Don Paco was invited with other friends to a celebration at Cela's home. A later internet search throws up a photo of the two men together and more detail on the life of Don Francisco Cortijo Ayuso. He was a well-known doctor and also an enthusiastic promoter of literature and culture, as well as being an advocate for Pastrana and the Alcarria. He did not remain deputy mayor; he became serving mayor of the town for over ten years between 1961 and 1971.

Cela and he clearly shared interests, an obvious work ethic, sharp intellects and a love of words. It was a friendship that began here in this square on a hot day in June, just like this one, nearly 80 years ago. It is a miniscule footnote in history but thrilling for just this moment to be in this place, speaking to this very warm and open lady and hearing these stories.

It feels like the conversation could continue for a lot longer but I don't want the energy to evaporate. I ask permission to keep her number and tell her I will send her a copy of the book. She offers to help with anything else I want to ask.

It has been a happy half hour full of anecdotes and detail that could only come from someone who knows.

It is lunchtime and I go back to the place where I had morning coffee. It has a stone floor and colourful, patterned tiles reaching halfway up the walls. The tables are wooden, solid and neatly presented with a linen tablecloth underneath a green paper top-layer table covering. The food I knew would be good in a way that Spanish food almost always is.

This is a place for a *"Menu del Día"*. That means a simple, uncomplicated choice from three or four starters, three or four main courses plus a drink, coffee and/or dessert or both if you wish, although you'll pay a bit more if you want both. The chalkboard outside announces today's offering:

Primeros
Ensalada mixta (Mixed salad)
Brocoli (Broccoli)
Gazpacho

Segundos
Lentejas (Lentils)
Merluza (Hake)
Filete de ternera (Steak)

The simplicity and symmetry of these words is practically sculptural to me, to say nothing of its deep understanding of human psychology and the paradox of choice. If only life's choices could be trimmed to this level of clarity. And behind the words on this chalkboard menu there is additional reassuring simplicity. When Spanish restaurants name a dish you know what you are going to get. A mixed salad will be lettuce, tomato, tuna, half a boiled egg and probably a bit of asparagus and sweetcorn. You will then dress it with a drizzle of olive oil and some vinegar and maybe a pinch of salt.

Broccoli will be broccoli. Gazpacho will be gazpacho. You get the idea.

There will be no hidden complexity. You can trust that what arrives at the table will be as written on the chalkboard. You can also trust that it will have come from a real kitchen with a real cook using real ingredients. Some places, of course, are better than others and you may not like any of it but you will not be able to complain that it was different to what was promised. If you stick to local dishes you will almost always eat well in Spain at this simple local restaurant level. Sometimes pasta dishes squeeze through the back door onto chalkboards. Avoid them. Pasta tends to get overboiled in this country. Beyond that, though, you have a long list of choices of simple, hearty dishes which will have you walking out happy, sated and still with enough money for your bus fare home or probably even a taxi. It will also have been a short and sweet experience. Limited choice means preparation time is short, service is brisk and table turnover is fast. That is the deal. It's priced at a level which is economically viable if there is a decent flow of customers. For many years, I used to have lunch with my girlfriend in a restaurant next to one of Madrid's main train stations. It was conveniently located for both of our workplaces and we could get there, eat, talk and get back to our separate workplaces in just over an hour. The eating bit could sometimes be reduced down to around 20 minutes including starter, main course and coffee. Romance *and* efficiency. It's a stellar combination.

Lean methodologies, achieving more with less, being more productive, and maxing out on efficiency are daily dietary staples for Ted talks, whizz bang industry conferences and board meetings all over the world. You can cover it all by selling your grandmother to raise the money to do a Business School MBA or you could just get down for some lunch at this restaurant and thousands more like it around Spain.

And by the way, my plate of broccoli was delicious, cooked with a bit of garlic.

After gazpacho and broccoli I am offered the dessert, *postre*. The conversation goes like this:

Waiter: *¿Algún postre?* (A dessert?)

Me: *¿Que hay?* (What is there?)

Waiter: *Hay flan, arroz con leche, natillas o fruta.* (We have crème caramel, cold rice pudding, custard or fruit)

Me: *¿Cual es la fruta?* (What fruit is it?)

Waiter: *Melón o sandía.* (Melon or watermelon.)

Me: *Melón, entonces. Gracias.* (Melon then. Thanks.)

(Waiter exits stage left toward kitchen)

It is a conversation repeated millions of times every day all over the country. The desserts rarely vary. You may be offered a *Tarta de Santiago*, which is a traditional Galician almond cake, or a cheesecake or perhaps some ice cream in the summer and the fruit will obviously vary depending on season. The core script, however, is written, slickly rehearsed and there are very few plot variations. I find these rituals comforting and life-affirming. It seems to me that in all of this there is centuries of human wisdom distilled into defining what works and what doesn't, what is good for us and what isn't, and what our priorities should be as we go about our daily lives.

After lunch I walk out again onto the square recalling other memories that I have of this place. There was a day nearly 20 years ago when I came with my young family. My son was about five years old and my daughter had just been born. I remember happy hours shelling out a steady flow of Euros to pay for him to go for ride after ride on bumper cars. The bumper cars were located where now there is a kiosk and café terrace. We believed at that time that he had a special gift for driving. Being so young he drove fast, with freedom, fearlessly dodging in and out of oncoming traffic. His pronounced shock of auburn hair bobbed and weaved, his face serious with concentration. When the cars stopped and the horn blew he'd come running towards me.

"Can I go again, Dad?"

"One more, but then we need to go."

"But, Dad. We don't really need to go, do we?"

So there we were later, our little travelling troupe in Pastrana, me pushing my daughter asleep in her pram, my ex walking and talking with my father while simultaneously dispensing short and long range motherly love and supervision.

It was just a year or so after my mother had died. My father was there in his role as Grandad, but I remember him very well later that afternoon gazing for a little too long at a lady serving coffee. For that brief visceral moment here in Pastrana he was the young man that he had been and not just the father he had become. He was dressed as always, an open necked beige cotton shirt, comfortable trousers, his shock of white hair thick on top and with narrow eyes. For that small instant in Pastrana I saw him like I never had before.

It is now very hot and the streets are empty. Soon it will be siesta time, the silence will deepen and this grand medieval city will slumber.

On the way back to the car I send a message to my son asking him if he remembers the bumper cars in Pastrana. He now lives in London, having gone to university in the UK and staying there after his school years in Spain.

Ten minutes later I get a ping in my pocket.

"No."

You ask the question. You get the answer.

There's a famous old quote in the advertising industry: "Half the money I spend on advertising is wasted; the trouble is I don't know which half." You could say the same about parenting. It's hard to know quite what the impact of all of our high-octane, high-minded parenting delivers in the long run. I'm not an expert. I am not a naturally gifted parent but my hunch is that our impact is not quite as significant as we would like it to be on the optimistic end of our expectation spectrum, nor is it as entirely irrelevant as we would wish it to be on the days when we fancy downing a bottle of red, collapsing on the sofa, smoking half a packet of Marlboros while listening to Billie Holliday records and being left alone, especially by the kids.

I thought that I was building happy lifetime memories spending long hours and a chunky proportion of my then-monthly salary on an extended bumper car session all those years ago. You know, those golden moments that get slowed down in the movies, when the protagonists flooded by sunlight go on carefree bike rides, run races on expansive sandy beaches, wipe smudges of milkshake off each other's noses, all before collapsing into a field of head-high golden wheat laughing deliriously. Most likely we did not create those types of memories. But there was a lot of love around that day. And one day he and my daughter may return to this place and maybe it will feel weirdly familiar to them and maybe they will sense afresh how they too are connected in unseen, profound and unconscious ways to people and to the places that they have been.

24 hours later

The lady at the entrance is smiling and seems genuinely happy to see me.

She is wearing a white coat rather like a lab technician or doctor might. Her hair is long and curly and she has dark enthusiastic eyes. She looks comfortable in the space and takes pleasure in explaining directions, key points to note and the best way of circulating around the building. I am looking to my right from the main entrance and I see a room full of display cases, panels on the wall and memorabilia.

I am already glad that I have travelled here to see this place.

There is a 1983 documentary on YouTube featuring Camilo José Cela on a visit here where he explains his intention to create a museum housing a life's collection of his writing memorabilia, first editions, notebooks, letters, original manuscripts, awards, photographs. He also suggests that this same village will be his final resting place.

The documentary is slow paced with long, fixed camera shots and a music track that has the kind of wobbly, warped, chewed-up cassette sound that you used to get on dodgy VHS tapes. It shows a rustic, agricultural Spain in a period of transition to a more efficient, productive agribusiness model. He speaks of a happy childhood, of never really wanting to become an adult. He shows his childhood home, walks along the railway track behind and explains how he has just bought a house in the village, at that time in need of total refurbishment, where he may one day return to live. For pulsating action and production values it is not a hit, but as historical record it is a beautiful film.

Iria Flavia, in Galicia, is over 600 kilometres from Madrid in Spain's far northwest corner and I have come here to see where Cela's journey began and ended.

The house that he bought became the headquarters of the *Camilo José Cela Galician Public Foundation*. The building has grown over the years with the slow acquisition of some of the adjoining houses, and is now big enough to house offices, an archive, a substantial museum and a conference room for cultural events.

As I walk through the museum it is how I imagine he would have liked it. It was inaugurated in 1991 and during his life Cela personally supervised the development of the collection. You can tell. It has an uncomplicated air. It is full of the things he envisioned: notebooks, publications, manuscripts, books, magazines, artwork, letters, photographs.

What is palpable is his overwhelming interest in the hard craft and daily practice of writing rather than the glory and recognition that can come with it. And there was plenty of glory, culminating in the Nobel Prize for Literature. The Nobel Prize gets coverage in the museum but doesn't obliterate the work. There is a video on loop of the ceremony in December 1989 when Cela was awarded the prize by the King of Sweden and the medal itself is on display. It is a thoughtful juxtaposition – a transient moment captured on film and the physical material left behind.

Even more evocative to me is the simple display of the rucksack he carried on his back when he went walking in the Alcarria. As I stand here, decades later in this quiet space, I can hear Cela's gruff voice in that bar in Pastrana drinking vermouth, eating olives and sharing stories with Don Paco, this very rucksack resting against a table leg at his feet.

I am not a reporter, nor historian nor academic. I have no wider view on Cela as a writer or where he belongs in the literary canon or what he represents in Spain as a cultural figure. I really don't care. His legacy for me was highly personal and is what I think is any writer's greatest achievement, to connect with a reader and make a genuine, long-lasting, life-enhancing impression. That connection is the miracle of words and why every time we pass a secondhand bookshop we should stop, go in and stand in awe of all that has ever been written and of those who took the time and trouble to write it. A lot won't appeal to us, some of it we won't understand, a lot of it is not very good but when we open a new book, we open our mind to something outside of ourselves and a voice enters our head that is not our own. And when our card beeps on the payment machine or we leave some cash on the counter, we participate in an act of cultural curation as important as that of any major museum. We are keeping ideas alive, finding those writers' ideas new homes to live in and new readers to connect with. We are choosing life not death.

We live in a time of polarised opinions, quick judgements and absolute absolutes where ideas can be demonised and killed off before they have time to breathe. I have seen my friend Raúl grimace when I mention Cela's name and he has explained why. Cela's style and attitudes appear to not chime with our times, or not at least with those that decide what the chimes should be. I don't have any metric or index to measure this but Cela's work may seem to be less read, less studied and less revered than it once was. In the cultural zeitgeist of today's Spain, let's just say that his face doesn't quite fit. For now, that is, because these waves of popular opinion come and go, just like we do. Thank God. It's why bookshops and libraries should remain and so should every single book ever written. They can survive long after us and our febrile, collective cultural and political mood-swings.

My vote goes for a plural society where we are free to contemplate an artist's work for what it is without feeling the need to make a judgement on the life they lived and their entire moral, political and sexual universe. Scratch the surface of any of us humans and you will find an indecipherable combination of contradictions, hypocrisies, random blind spots and stupidity. I'm happy to admit it, or at least some of it. You?

Most dangerous of all, I reckon, are those that think they don't share some or all of these most human characteristics. More than a blind spot, it's a cosmic black hole.

Meanwhile, back in the Spanish cultural turf wars, I have a secret weapon.

As an immigrant to this country when conversation heats up at dinner parties and family lunches over national or regional politics, I have the inbuilt and highly advantageous functionality of stone-cold neutrality. I just don't have the visceral genetic and cultural connections to the many issues that mean so much to so many people. It's not because I don't understand them or that I'm not interested. I am very interested and I have opinions (sometimes) but I usually keep them to myself. It's just a question of blood ties and birthright tribal allegiances and I don't have them in Spain.

By contrast, if you tank me up with a few beers and bring up the subject of the Disneyfication of London's West End or the comparative media blackout on Crystal Palace FC you will quickly see my thermostat rocketing.

Air

On the road outside heavy traffic thunders by. It is an unwelcome soundtrack for what is a very pretty rural village vista. If this were an internet video I would turn the sound down. Maybe when we are all hanging out in the metaverse we will have that option, as virtual overlaps with reality, but for today I must simply wait.

After a minute or two there is a gap in the traffic and I cross the road to the *Iglesia de Santa María*. It is in this church where Cela was baptised and was buried in its cemetery in 2002.

Set back from the road and behind the church the traffic noise is less invasive. I can now hear the sound of my feet crunching across the little white pebbles and shells that mark the paths. The graves are well kept, clean and many have fresh flowers. The sun shines down casting angular shadows and there is a very soft breeze, cool for this morning in June.

Two ladies are attending to graves. One is wearing black shorts and a white T-shirt and is bent over replacing wilted flowers with freshly picked ones. She does it slowly and with unhurried precision.

Cela's resting place is at the edge of the cemetery under an olive tree. It is simple, no grander than any other. I am just a few hundred metres from the house where he grew up. From where I am standing, I can see the house that he bought and the foundation dedicated to maintaining his collection. I can imagine him as a young boy looking down the railway track across the road with his desire to travel awakened, and I can imagine that same young boy in an older man's body wanting to come home. Perhaps this is the story. Of how we all go travelling and of how we return home, wherever or whatever that is.

Because, after official commemorations and accolades are forgotten, there will be a soul in a grand city somewhere in the world who will walk into a bookshop on an otherwise unremarkable day and discover Cela on a shelf somewhere amidst the colourful book spines. And maybe they will also be dazzled and inspired.

And that may just be the starting point for another journey.

The sea

The A6 is a motorway that starts in Madrid right by the Presidential palace of La Moncloa and heads northwest to Galicia. I have driven up and down its first congested stretch thousands of times over the years in my daily loop of life.

It's called the *La Carretera de la Coruña* (the Coruña road) and the name of that distant Galician city is present on top of all the signage every kilometre of the way. It is the final destination that few ever reach, not being a place you pass through on the way to anywhere else.

But on those days when you're tired of the world and you just want to put your foot to the floor, push hard, keep going and get away, *La Coruña* becomes an ever-present shorthand for freedom. It promises Atlantic winds, cooler temperatures and an infinite view.

I went there once, some years ago. I remember that hotel with a beautiful glass frontage and views out to sea on a long weekend of books and walks. Today I've come again to see where this magical land meets the sea.

I walk east, heading away from the city, following the coast, past the city beach, up the hill until the buildings thin and there is a clear view of the Hercules Tower, the lighthouse standing high on a headland. The wind is now picking up beyond the lighthouse and I settle to sit on an expansive green-grassed clifftop. The Atlantic wind is blowing strong and the waves break hard on the rocks below. Charging white surf collides with sparkling blue as it has done forever. Again and again the water comes and marks the insistent, eternal rhythm that is never broken.

Where better to rest before a long road home?

To share a thought, opinion or enquiry:
djmbjm@gmail.com